MAGGIE'S
Refrain

MAGGIE'S Refrain

FULL CIRCLE - BOOK II

BY

MARCIA WARE

WordCrafts

Published by WordCrafts Press
Buffalo, WY 37388
www.wordcrafts.net

Dedication

To Grandma, Daddy, Mom, Margaret, Maria and Alan...
where the circle began.

To David, Lily, Andrew and Addison...
where the circle completes.

And to my Savior, who holds us all together.

Family is everything.

Chapter 1

The Yuletide season brought with it the hustle and bustle that was common for the Buchanan Family. But without Grace's energetic sense of order, it never took long for Joe to feel the pressure of being all things to all people. There were school pageants and church musicals, cookie baking, house decorating, gift buying, and of course, Christmas break for the kids. And with the semester at the University winding down, Joe was faced with the daunting task of gearing up for finals and grading tomes of term papers.

If not for the ready assistance he received from the women in his life - his mother Elise, Sissy and Maggie - Joe's world would have spun into a whirlwind of inescapable confusion.

Elise offered to take the twins off of his hands for a weekend with promises of shopping for presents, pictures with Santa, and all the Christmas treats she could pump into their little bodies.

"May God have mercy on your soul," Joe chuckled as he watched his mother's car drive away with the twins that morning. For her part, Joe knew Elise was a loving grandmother who divided her discipline and her diversions evenly. If anyone could handle Matty and Mary Margaret, it was she.

Sissy made plans to have Gwen stay at her place for

some fun "girl time." Joe couldn't remember ever having seen his daughter so excited. Bubbling over with eager anticipation, Gwen practically tackled her aunt as Sissy came through the door.

"Are you sure you're up for this," Joe asked.

"Oh yeah," said Sissy, peeling Gwen off of her arm in order to pull some DVDs from her stylish designer backpack.

While Grace might have been the accomplished artist, Sissy was definitely the arbiter of fashion in the Hammond family. One would never guess that she was born a Midwestern girl. Her wardrobe choices were 100 percent Rodeo Drive.

She was never one to simply "throw something together." It was all carefully and meticulously planned, from the jeweled sunglasses that held back her thick, radiant hair, right down to the soles of her Italian leather boots. Whenever she knew she'd be seeing Joe, she always played up the glamour just a little bit more. And Joe, being a man, would always notice. He had never denied his sister in law's statuesque beauty.

"Wow Sis, you look great," he said.

Still searching for the DVDs, Sissy gave a flirtatious toss of the head and smiled. "Thanks," she replied.

"So, whatcha got planned for my baby?"

Having found the movies, Sissy put her arm around Gwen. "Well, after I get my sweet niece home and settled in, there's an afternoon tea for Women in the Entertainment Arts, at the Opryland hotel. Gwen, I would love for you to be my guest."

Gwen nodded an enthusiastic "Yes!"

"Then I thought we'd pay a little visit to my office at Star - thought I'd show you what I get to do all day."

Joe was impressed. "Ooh, can I go too?"

"Dad," Gwen sighed.

"I know, I know...no boys allowed," Joe said, pretending to be disappointed.

"A *private* tour for you next time," Sissy whispered with a wink.

Joe wasn't quite sure what he was meant to do with her response, so he simply smiled politely. "Sounds like you've got a lot going on," he said.

"Oh, but I'm not done," Sissy said brightly. "I thought we'd have dinner at Margot." Turning her attention to Gwen, she asked, "Have you ever had French food?"

Wide-eyed, the young girl shook her head. "Then Margot it is!" Sissy said triumphantly. "Then I thought we'd close out the evening with some serious chick flicks. How's that sound?"

Gwen bit her lip; using every ounce of energy she could to maintain composure, because she could tell Sissy had more.

"Now tomorrow, we've got breakfast at Loveless Café..."

"From Margot to the Loveless cafe," Joe said. "Impressive."

"I'm a firm believer in mixing it up," Sissy cooed. "As I was saying, after that, a full day of shopping and pampering at the spa."

Then it was time to reveal the part of the plan she knew her niece wanted to hear. "The shopping part is very important because we're going to...wait for it..." A final reach inside of her bag yielded what appeared to be two large tickets. With a look of pride she announced, "...The big Star Records Christmas party downtown at the Renaissance Hotel!"

Feeling as though she'd won the lottery, Gwen was

ready to come out of her skin. "Aunt Sissy, you are the *bomb!*"

"That means she thinks you're cool," Joe said knowledgeably.

"I think I got that," Sissy laughed.

"Oh, swag *money!*" Gwen cheered while simultaneously pulling her cell out of her pocket and jumping up and down. "I can't wait to text my BF Jess to tell her I'm gonna turn up with DT at the Star Jam…she is gonna freak!"

Joe and Sissy met with blank stares.

"Ohhkay. I got nothin'," said Joe.

"I'm gonna assume it's still something good…?" Sissy asked, her eyes conveying an expression of hopefulness.

Furiously sending out a message on her phone, Gwen laughed. "Of course it is," she said. "I'm telling Jess that I'll finally get to meet Deana at the Star party, and Jess is gonna be really excited."

Snapping his fingers, Joe said, "I have *got* to get that English to Teenage Translator."

Apparently finished flaunting her good fortune to her friend, Gwen returned her phone to her pocket. "So what movies did you get, Aunt Sissy," asked Gwen, finally taking a breath.

Sissy beamed with pride. "I got *Kit Kittredge* and *The Little Mermaid!*"

Gwen looked as if she'd been doused with cold water. "Are you kidding me? What am I, ten?"

Sissy appeared to be shocked. "You mean, you don't like what I picked out?"

Gwen immediately recognized her faux pas. "Oh, I'm sorry, Aunt Sissy," she said, embarrassed. "I didn't mean to…"

"I just can't believe this! I went through all of the

trouble to find movies I thought you'd like, and I'm just so hurt!"

Gwen began to wonder into what kind of weekend she was walking. She turned to look at her father, hoping he might give her some sort of help. Joe stared at the ground, lips pursed, but there was no denying he wanted to laugh out loud.

"Gotcha!" Sissy exclaimed.

Gwen blushed as she let out a sound of relief. "Ha ha ha, very funny," she said. "Okay seriously, what did you really get?"

Sissy showed her the side panel of the DVD case. "*Pride and Prejudice…*"

"The one with Keira Knightley?"

"You got it!"

Gwen screamed and said something completely indecipherable. Joe winced and put a finger in his ear.

"I'd ask what the other movie is, but I'm afraid that I'll lose my hearing completely," he said.

Sissy revealed the other title. "I got…*13 going on 30!*"

Gwen continued to cheer as Joe continued to shield his ears from the noise.

"I'm off to learn sign language. I'm officially impaired," he joked. Kissing Gwen on her forehead, he added, "Alright then, hug your father and scram. He's got work to do."

With the kids officially occupied and the house silent, Joe dove into his tasks with a steady determination. By the time he came up for air, the clock read 7:30 pm.

He decided to take a break and fix himself a sandwich when there was a knock at the back door. It was Maggie. He couldn't tell what she was wearing beneath her coat, but from the look of her hair and makeup, it was clear she was planning to do something special. In one hand she carried her purse, in the other, an oversized gift bag.

"Merry Christmas!" she said as he opened the door. "I know you're really busy, but I thought maybe you could use a break."

Genuinely glad to see her, he stepped aside to let her in. "Hey you, perfect timing," he said. "As a matter of fact, I was just fixing..." His words trailed off as Maggie playfully pushed past him on her way to the living room, pretending to ignore him.

"Sure, come on in, make yourself at home," he said with feigned incredulity. "As I was saying, I'm fixing myself something to eat. Wanna join me in some fried bologna?"

Maggie removed her coat to reveal a wrap-around dress of deep eggplant that complimented her curves and emphasized the best of her shape. Her hair was pulled away from her face by a brown suede headband that allowed her curls to cascade fully around her shoulders. Her knee-high boots matched the headband, and her makeup and jewelry were subtle and understated.

"Wow," Joe said. "That's not a sandwich dress."

Despite his attempt at humor, Joe's admiration was evident, sending Maggie's confidence skyward. Following his lead, she casually tossed her coat on a nearby chair. "Precisely. Especially not *fried bologna*," she said haughtily.

"Elitist."

"I'm a Spam girl, what can I tell you?"

"Duly noted."

"Besides, you'd burn it anyway."

"True."

"I mean, for real. I've seen you burn water."

"Okay!" he laughed. "Point taken. Now, moving on to

more important things..." Attempting to look inside the bag, he asked with a mischievous, childlike tone, "What'd ya bring me...?"

Maggie began to remove several beautifully wrapped boxes from the bag, placing them under the tree. "Well, Mr. I'm-the-Center-of-the-Universe, there are *several* gifts in here, if you must know. Yes, here's something for you..."

"I knew it."

"Boy, hush. Here are the ones for the kids. This one's for your mom, and I even got Sissy and the Hammonds something."

"You have got to be the most impressive little elf I've ever seen," he said. "Can I open mine now?"

Maggie gave him a look that was clearly meant to discourage. "Alright, alright," he said. "But I can't promise I won't open it after you go home."

"Well, that's between you and Kris Kringle," she said.

"Do you have a hot date tonight? You look fantastic."

"Thank you. No hot date, but I do have an agenda." As she folded the large gift bag, she proceeded to unveil her plan. "I've got a really sweet friend, a fellow singer named Kira, and we do session work around town together. She's doing her thing down at Sambuca tonight with some cool arrangements on Christmas songs..."

"Say no more. Give me 10 minutes. I would love to get out of here," he said.

As he sprinted up the stairs, Maggie took a moment to regard the Christmas tree. She noticed a silver box wedged between some of the branches, the gift tag bearing her name.

"Can I take my Christmas present?" she yelled up the stairs.

Joe rummaged through his closet with urgent

intensity. Holding various items out at arm's length, he muttered, "Nah, she's seen me in that already..."

Catching himself before declaring that a particular pair of khakis made his backside look odd, he laughed, shook his head and settled on black jeans and a rich, olive-green cable knit sweater.

He heard Maggie yell something from downstairs, but couldn't make out what she was saying. He figured she was telling him to hurry up, so he began to pick up his pace.

There were bottles and tubes of styling product on the sink in the bathroom that he'd purchased at Gwen's urging, thinking that maybe he could do something different with his hair - something that his daughter deemed a bit more 'modern.'

"Your hair is so retro," she would say. "I mean, it's cool that you have long hair, 'cause it's in - but you're a dad; you need 'dad' hair."

Whatever "dad" hair actually was, he promised her he'd consider it someday. But for now, Joe settled within himself that this evening would probably not be the best time to experiment. "Better leave well enough alone," he said. The way it naturally fell around his face once his hands went through was all the grooming he figured he'd need.

Chapter 2

Donning a leather jacket, Joe froze in his tracks for one final review. A spray of cologne - *not too much; don't wanna overpower her*-and he was ready.

Sambuca was a perfect choice. Kira was in rare form, mixing the promised holiday tunes with jazz standards and gritty soul and blues. Halfway through her second set, she called Maggie up to sing a song or two. With a little urging, Maggie grabbed a stool and a microphone, and let the music take her where it wanted to go.

She sat poised and lovely as she took her place on the stage. Bathed in the spotlight, she was luminous. Joe had to remind himself to breathe. He felt a burning in the center of his chest that made it impossible for him to sit completely still. A sense of pride coursed through him, however, when he was able to see the effect that Maggie's voice had on everyone else in the room.

As the crowd cheered at the end of a tender duet between the women, Joe jumped up to help Maggie down from her place on the stage and back to their table. The emotion of the moment was palpable. The music swirled around them and drew them in as Joe tenderly took Maggie's hand in his own.

The ride home was, for the most part, silent. When they did speak, they kept it around the edges of what seemed to be on both of their minds.

"So…Kira seemed really cool. I enjoyed talking with her too," he said.

"Yeah, she's a genuine talent. One of the best."

"One of," Joe agreed. "But I'm telling you, you're still my favorite. You were amazing tonight. Everyone loved you. I think you stole the show."

Maggie turned to Joe and smiled. He glanced over just long enough to drink it in. He reached out and took her hand.

She spent the rest of the drive staring down at the two sets of fingers intertwined. Her delicate tan hand fit nicely in his, their skin tones not too terribly far apart. Joe took his thumb and ran it back and forth over hers in that earth shaking way that lets a person know that they truly enjoy being in close physical contact. The sensation sent Maggie's stomach spinning.

Neither of them wanted to let go.

At the house, Joe and Maggie lingered in the car for as long as they could, but they knew that their evening was coming to an end. Joe broke the silence, by asking, "So, you fly home for Christmas with your family tomorrow?"

"Yeah, the flight's at 6 pm."

"Seems a bit early. Christmas isn't for another week."

"Things have been going well with Daddy and me. I just want to spend more time with him."

"That's great, Maggie. I'm really happy for you. You need a lift to the airport?"

"Nah, thanks, I've got that covered. Deana wants us to lay down some bgv's on the new album, and she wants to get the bulk of it done before we all scatter to the winds. Darla's gonna drop me off."

Joe furrowed his brow. "Lay down some bgv's?"

Maggie smiled, "Record background vocals."

For the second time that day, Joe found it ironic that his mastery of the English language was being challenged yet again. "You crazy musicians with your own language," he teased. "But since we're on the subject - I have always wanted to see how you do what you do."

"You're welcome to come," she said. "In fact, I'd love it if you did."

She pulled a business card out of her purse and began to write down directions to the studio. "I'll tell the guys to be on the lookout for you. There's always someone up front; just tell them you're a friend of mine, and they'll take you back to the proper room."

Joe was excited. "Thanks Mags. This is so amazing! I can't wait."

"And on that note…"

"Very 'punny.' Come on, I'll walk you to your car."

She allowed Joe time to come around on her side to let her out. They rejoined hands as they made the slow walk back to her SUV.

The night was cool, but not cold; typical of that time of year in Nashville. But neither Joe nor Maggie felt the chill.

She leaned against her car, her hand still in Joe's. Joe gazed deeply into Maggie's eyes and inhaled sharply. Slowly, he released her hand, and enveloped her with both arms. She returned the gesture by wrapping her arms around his neck. Before long, their hug began to morph into a slow dance, swaying back and forth to the music that resonated in their heads.

With one arm still around her waist, Joe reached up and grabbed Maggie's other hand. He led her in a silent waltz, his eyes never leaving hers as the emotion between them grew steadily.

As he twirled her around, Maggie laughed her intoxicating laugh. He smiled as he drew her back into his arms.

Joe realized that this was the moment: The crossroads he'd both feared and fantasized. If he didn't do something now, he might never have the nerve to ever try again. And that was something he couldn't bear to imagine.

His heart practically bursting through his ribcage, Joe lifted his hands to her face, leading her to the point of no return.

Tentative at first, within the next few heartbeats, Joe and Maggie felt their self-consciousness dissolve. His hands in her hair, her arms under his, Maggie clung to Joe as they drank deeply from this well that they'd discovered together; never realizing until that moment how desperately thirsty they both were.

She felt a tear of longing roll down her cheek. This kiss was affecting her, body and soul. It was an awakening, a gift and a miracle...happening to the two of them in a season that is full of such things.

Suddenly, a gust of wind hit them both - a chill that brought with it a familiar shadow moving past. The realization made itself heard:

This is my best friend's husband...

This is my wife's best friend...

"Oh no!" Maggie cried as she pushed herself away.

"Maggie..." Joe began.

Her hand moved to her mouth, the flesh of her lips still vibrating from his kiss. "I'm so sorry, Joe. I don't know what came over me..."

"No, Maggie, it was me. I stepped over the line..."

"I've got to go."

"Maggie, wait!"

"Joe, I can't…I'm sorry! Good night!"

He stood in the drive until the red of her tail lights disappeared around the bend into the night. Squeezing his eyes shut, he tried to compartmentalize his fear, guilt and desire to make some sense of what had just happened.

It was the sound of the telephone in the distance that moved him from his frozen state. Reaching it on the last ring before it was lost to voice mail, he answered, slightly breathless.

"A little late to be running a marathon, isn't it?"

Joe looked down at the caller ID. It was Sissy.

He tried to sound cheerful. "Hey there-how's girls' weekend going?"

"Great! Gwennie's sacked out next to me here on the couch. You okay?"

His mind still in the driveway, still kissing Maggie, Joe didn't answer right away.

"Joey? You okay?"

"Sorry, Sis. Yeah, I'm good. It's been a long day buried in papers."

"Have you even eaten? Do you need anything?"

"I did. Maggie came by, and we went out for a while."

Sissy closed her eyes in disgust and softly drew in her breath before saying, "You and Maggie again, huh?"

Still distracted, he didn't pick up on what she was trying to convey. "Uh huh," he said. "We went downtown to hear a friend of hers sing. It was good."

Silent for a few seconds before deciding to speak her mind, Sissy finally managed to ask, "Is there something we should know about you two?"

Joe finally heard the direction in which she was driving the conversation. "Maggie and I have been friends for years, Sis. You know that."

"Friends, sure…but all of this time she's been spending over there when she's not out singing, then she broke up with that guy she was seeing. I'm simply saying it feels a little suspect."

An exasperated sigh. "'Suspect,' Sissy?"

She knew she was on potentially shaky ground. She tried to choose her words carefully.

"I know it's been nearly two years since Gracie, um, well, I just don't want to see you get caught up in some big emotional thing."

The conflict that waged within him over the kiss, combined with Sissy's inquisition and his general fatigue was more than he could handle at that moment. Leaning against the wall, he shut his eyes as she continued her complaint.

"What I'm trying to say is, as your family…as someone who cares about you…as the sister of your *wife*, I feel as though it's my responsibility to…"

"First of all, *Gwyneth*," Joe interjected. "As the *sister* of my wife, you are fulfilling your responsibility by extending the love and care that you've given to the kids and me since Grace passed away."

The button had been pushed. She knew she had gone too far. Joe never called her by her Christian name. She began to try and justify her concerns. "Yes, but…"

"Secondly, as I mentioned before, Maggie has been a daily fixture in my world for nearly twenty years. We've always been close, always been able to communicate well with one another. I don't know if things are changing. I'm not really able to understand it all right now. But even if I did, I owe you absolutely, positively *no* explanation. Are we clear?"

Sissy sat silently, gazing down at Gwen, who

continued to sleep on the couch beside her. Finally, she managed to say, "Crystal. I'm sorry Joe. I didn't mean to offend you."

"Oh, I'm sorry too," he said, running his free hand through his hair. "This has been a long day, and I think my mental hard drive is full."

"Time to reboot?" she said with compassion.

Joe stretched and yawned. "You know it."

Sissy chuckled. "You know, the reason I called was just to see if you needed anything. I simply wanted to check up on you. Sorry that it turned into something tense."

"Listen Sis, Maggie and me…we're friends. She's been there for me through the darkest time of my life. I think the world of her. I believe in her. She's a good person. But don't read too much into anything…" He stopped before he found himself in a lie. Then he said, "I loved Grace. I always will. But I'm just now getting my arms around the fact that I am a single man again. It is not my intention to get involved in some 'big emotional thing,' as you put it, with anyone at this point."

Despite the sinking feeling he was experiencing at that moment over Maggie, it was as honest as he knew to be. And it was enough to lift the cloud from Sissy's spirit immediately.

"Thanks for calling, hon," he said. I'm gonna head to bed now. Take care of my little girl, and have fun tomorrow."

"No problem, Joey. Thanks for entrusting her to me. G'night."

Bending down to unplug the Christmas tree lights before heading to bed, Joe saw his gift from Maggie. His curiosity got the better of him; he grabbed it and took it with him to his room. He placed the box on the edge of the bed and proceeded to pace back and forth; periodically picking it up, and then putting it back down. After several minutes' deliberation, he drew in a breath and exhaled slowly, his fingers mid-rake through his hair.

The thoughts came with lightening speed: The magic of the evening at Sambuca, the kiss, the argument...the contents of that confounded box. He chose to ignore his stress and headed to the shower.

Emerging from the bathroom, Joe chuckled at the box's solitary state at the edge of the bed; almost as if it were patiently waiting for his return. Annoyed by his own childish behavior, he made a direct line for the box and tore it open. *For Pete's sake, what is the big deal?* he scolded himself as he removed the satin ribbon and the lid in one smooth motion.

Joe lifted the sterling silver bracelet from the box, and immediately put it on. It looked good on his arm.

"Really good taste, Mags," he said softly.

Discarding the paper and bow, he picked up the box and placed it on the nightstand. A small piece of paper that had been stuck to the inside of the lid of the box floated quietly to the floor. Joe picked it up and read what Maggie had written:

> *Everything comes full circle*
> *It falls together in the end*
> *The unshakable truth that saved my life*
> *Is that you are my best friend*
> *So I'm gonna run straight to ya*
> *Wind at my back face toward the sun*
> *Step inside my circle*
> *'Cause something wonderful has begun.*

He read and re-read the lyrics, remembering a

moment not so long ago when Maggie had sung those very words from the piano downstairs. Had she been writing about him all this time?

He then placed the paper on top of the box, and reclined on a stack of pillows on the bed. Staring at the chain on his wrist, he spent the rest of the night counting the potential cost of taking one such step inside that circle.

Chapter 3

S leep didn't come easily for Maggie that night, either. Developing feelings for a man who had been such a stalwart friend to her over the years seemed unthinkable. Kissing him? Even further from the scope of her reality.

From the outside looking in, the road couldn't have led to any other place. Joe and Maggie were inexorably bound together...by friendship, by his children...ultimately, by Grace. And in Maggie's mind this was *not* the way to honor her memory.

She groaned in agony as she pulled a pillow over her head, berating herself for being so transparent so soon.

"What in the world have I done?"

Still unable to sleep at 3 am, she went downstairs for a drink of water. Vacillating between guilt and euphoria, Maggie sat in her favorite spot on the couch and stared out the window. It was all still fresh in the forefront of her mind: the pressure of Joe's caress around her torso; his lips on hers. Tears mixed with girlish laughter at the memory of holding his hand, dancing in the dark and his otherworldly embrace.

It was then that Maggie remembered the box. Her Christmas present from Joe was still in her car. Barefoot, she carefully tip-toed to the passenger side and retrieved

Maggie laughed aloud when she saw the familiar name of the department store emblazoned across the top. It was the same store where she'd purchased Joe's wrist chain.

"Apparently great minds think alike," she said.

Inside the box was a necklace: Several tear-shaped onyx with tiny rhinestones around their edges, connected to a rhinestone strand with earrings to match. She picked it up and gasped in appreciation as the light from outside her window brought a brilliance to the stones.

There was also a small card that read,

Just because you're not famous yet doesn't mean you can't dress the superstar's part. Shine on, Maggie. Your day in the sun is coming.
Merry Christmas

Love, Joe.

Maggie warmed at the thought of him searching from store to store; perhaps getting help from Gwen or even his mother, not resting until he found just the right gift. Although it was costume, the necklace and earrings symbolized much more than monetary value.

Maggie knew this in her heart of hearts, and that alone made it priceless to her.

Chapter 4

Maggie might appear to be the picture of professionalism behind the microphone, but on the inside, her nerves were waging war. After two hours in the studio, Joe had yet to arrive. She decided that perhaps his fear had gotten the better of him and he decided to stay away.

Despite her initial remorse over the kiss she still wanted to see him, to thank him for his indescribably beautiful gift; to see if perhaps what the two of them experienced the night before could lead to somewhere wonderful.

It seemed as though for the first time in her life, Maggie was experiencing true affection for someone in earnest. For the first time in her life, if she could wade through the murky waters of guilt, maybe she could actually feel something incredibly close to hope.

Maybe…

Darla studied Maggie during a break as she watched her friend absentmindedly put one too many packets of artificial sweetener in her tea.

"Okay," she said, taking the Styrofoam cup from Maggie's hand. "You can't sing if you're drinking syrup, sweetheart. What's going on?"

"Huh? Oh, nothing. I was just…um…" Maggie said, still distracted.

Darla knew it was something, but decided to proceed with caution. "Hmmm…well, looks like we're going back in, so let me just dump this cup out, and get you some real tea."

Maggie looked at the six blue paper packets in her hand and realized what she'd done.

"Oh wow, gosh. Thanks," she said softly, handing everything over to Darla.

"Sweetie, I don't think I've ever seen you like this," Darla said. "What's going on?"

Maggie let out a heavy sigh. A tear began to form and fall over her lower lash. "I had the best and worst night of my life last night."

Darla looked over Maggie's shoulder to gauge how much time they had before Charles began barking at the stragglers. She decided they had a moment to spare. Maggie looked into Darla's face while wiping away the errant tear. "Wanna talk about it on the way to the airport later?" Darla asked.

Maggie sniffed and smiled. "Sure."

"Good-because if it's enough to work you up like this, then there have got to be some *seriously* juicy details involved," Darla cracked.

Maggie chuckled. "Girl, please," she said.

"Alright people," Charles was heard to say from somewhere down the hall. "Let's hop to it. Time is money!"

Both Maggie and Darla mouthed "Time is Money" at the exact same time that Charles had said it. Arm in arm, they laughed and made their way back to the recording booth.

Joe felt the same nervousness in his own stomach as he made his way down the corridor to the room where Maggie was working. For the longest time, he sat in his car, wrestling with whether or not he should go inside. But as he looked down at the chain on his wrist, he knew there was no way he couldn't be there. He couldn't let her leave town without at the very least confronting the situation that lay before them.

On the one hand, he was scared that Sissy was right. Perhaps was too soon after Grace's death for him to get into some "big emotional thing." Maybe this would be too much for the families to take: The Hammonds seeing their daughter being replaced…by her best friend, of all people. Sure, the children love her, but to see her in any role other than Aunt Maggie? He was acutely aware of the fact that they might not be able to get their young minds around it.

On the other hand, for the first time since Grace's death Joe couldn't escape the fact that he was starting to feel an intense healing. And there was no denying Maggie's presence played an enormous role in that. For the first time in a long while, he felt a sense of virility and vitality that he thought had been buried with his wife.

Maybe it was too soon to call it love; but maybe it was, in fact, the perfect time to discover exactly what it just might be.

Maybe…

He followed the music down a narrow hallway then down some stairs to a large, dimly lit room that was dominated by a massive sound board. Tweaking knobs and subtly adjusting levers, Charles turned from his work to acknowledge Joe's entrance and shake his hand. He offered Joe an available chair in a back corner as he whispered, "We're just about done; you almost missed it."

Joe smiled and nodded as he took his seat. There were several others in the room, including a man who sat next to Charles at the board. Periodically, the two would lean their heads toward one another to converse, but everyone else in the room was silent.

On the other side of an enormous window that stretched from floor to ceiling, Joe saw three men, and three women, including Maggie. They stood in groups of two in front of three separate microphones. Some had headphones covering both ears; some had one ear covered and the other exposed. They sat on stools or stood on tattered Oriental rugs that spread over hardwood floors.

Rich, thick fabric that served both acoustic and aesthetic purposes hung from sections of the colorful walls and vaulted ceiling. Antique wrought iron candelabras stood in various parts of the room to provide a soothing ambiance.

The singers' harmonies were glorious as they wrapped around Deana's simple scratch vocals. Joe marveled at how the engineers could simply push a button and in a moment's time, anything that might have been sung incorrectly was erased in a seamless transition. He was amazed at how they could perform the same passages over and over again in order to create the sound of a choir three times their size.

Caught up in the shared excitement of the control room, Joe found himself smiling broadly, and he nearly applauded at the song's triumphant conclusion.

"Alright guys and gals, that was fantastic," said Charles. "That's gonna do it for everybody but Maggie. I want to do some quick ad-libs on this last song."

The other singers exited the room and left Maggie

alone at her microphone. "Okay, hon," said Charles, "I need to tell you a thing. We're gonna roll the track, and you just do what you do."

The music began, and Maggie closed her eyes. Five seconds into her take, Maggie was able to cast off any constraints of tension she might have felt. She was home, completely in her element. As the sounds emerged whole and full from her throat, the entire room unleashed a symphony of sounds that signified the one fact that was never in doubt: Maggie was a true phenomenon.

Placing embellishments wherever she felt appropriate, building from soft, yet passionate tones to huge, gospel-infused bombast, the "ride" that Joe once described as Maggie's voice was taking everyone in that room to heights and depths that left them breathless.

Joe watched as she commandeered the journey. His heart warmed not only by what he was hearing but also by the beautiful vessel from which it came, Joe felt a sudden rush of inspiration.

Quietly making his way back to the hallway, he asked an abundantly tattooed young man where he could find Darla Dayton. The kid pointed behind him to the smaller of two women leaning against the wall engaged in light conversation.

"Darla," he asked.

She was willing to bet her next paycheck that this handsome guy standing in front of her was the source of Maggie's distraction. "Yeah," she said with a smile. "You're Joe, aren't you?"

Joe was afraid of any negative conversation that might have concerned him. "Yeah," he said sheepishly.

"Don't get your knickers in a twist, all I know is good stuff about you," Darla said with a wink.

Joe blushed.

"And there's no need to worry. Girlfriend's had her poker face on for the most part all day," she said. "But I'm not gonna lie; she's been a bit diverted. Said something about having the best and worst night of her life last night?" Her intonation of the end of the phrase bent upwards, as if she was hoping to glean some information from him.

Joe smiled and said, "Well, I don't, um...*date*...and tell." He punctuated his sentence with a wink of his own.

"You're a stinker. I like that in a man."

Joe laughed at the flirtatious moxie of the petite blonde. "I know you're taking Maggie to the airport today, but I was wondering if I could talk to you about surprising her at the airport when she gets back."

Darla was touched. Particularly in light of the slight despair she'd seen in Maggie's eyes. "I think she'd love that," she said with genuine graciousness. "I'll not say a word."

Just then, a muffled round of cheers could be heard from within the control room. The door opened, and various ones exited, with Charles saying, "Girl, you are the Queen of the one-take! Good Job, honey."

"Guess they're done," said Joe.

"She's got a few minutes before we have to head out," said Darla. She handed him a slip of paper. "Here's her return flight info. Go talk to her. I know she'd love to see you."

"Thanks Darla. It was nice to meet you."

"You too, sugar." As he walked away, she looked at the woman standing next to her with whom she'd been chatting. Both of them offered low whistles of appreciation.

Joe waded through a sea of individuals to make his back to Maggie. He stopped at the doorway and saw her chatting amiably with a tall, handsome African-American man. Joe couldn't tell what they were saying, but if he went only by body language, it would seem that they had a very familiar level of comfort with one another. The young man grasped her hand and she responded by covering her remaining hand over his.

As Maggie and Joe locked eyes, he felt his own initial fears and ambivalence return. He managed a smile and strode across the room with manufactured confidence. "You were amazing, Mags," he said as he reached her.

Maggie felt a rush of excitement shoot through every corner of her body as she reached out to take his hand. "Joe, I want you to meet Jared Fox," she said. "Jared, this is Joe Buchanan."

From his waist-length, immaculately styled locs to his ripped jeans, threadbare pashmina and faded bomber jacket, Jared Fox looked every inch the quintessential artist. As Joe extended his hand, he inwardly chuckled at the idea that this was someone Grace would have found fascinating on sight. He could hear Grace go on and on about how she 'dug his rock star vibe,' and how he'd be perfect for Maggie.

In that moment, Joe was reluctantly inclined to agree.

Jared's smile immediately illuminated the features on his boyish brown face. "Very nice to meet you," he said with a strong baritone. "Maggie, I'll talk to you later. Are we still on for dinner when you get back?"

"Absolutely. Merry Christmas."

"Merry Christmas. To both of you," he said as he answered his ringing cell phone.

Joe gave Jared a polite nod.

After saying goodbye to Charles and acknowledging the compliments of the other musicians as they passed by,

Joe and Maggie made their way out to Darla's car.

"I wonder where she is," said Maggie, looking around. "Oh well, she knows what time we have to leave. Did you enjoy yourself today? How much of it did you see?"

Joe hair was instantly flipped away from his face as he stood in the direction of the wind. He was no longer able to hide the mounting disappointment he was feeling and his expression began to darken. "I caught the last song, and that deal you did at the end. Like I said, you were absolutely awesome."

Maggie noticed the shift. "Thanks," she said tentatively. "What's wrong?"

Joe stared down at the ground and transferred his weight from foot to foot, partly due to the chill that the wind had brought, and partly from nervous apprehension.

"Maggie," he began.

Maggie's heart began to sink. It was an all too familiar tone: A tone that for her had always preceded a supreme letdown.

It was the tone a 13 year old boy in her science class used just before he discouraged her in his gauche teenage way from having a crush on him because he thought she was fat and ugly.

It was the tone that three different gospel labels had right before they told her how great she sounded, but felt that she didn't have the image to promote a successful singing career.

It was the tone Charles had used when she told him she still had dreams of branching out on her own.

Bracing herself once again, she immediately noticed how much more adept she was at handling the moment the older she became. Perhaps by this point, she was simply numb. She looked him squarely in the eye.

"Yes, Joe?" she said without an ounce of weakness.

Joe felt himself losing ground, and struggled to rally. He said her name again. "Maggie…"

Maggie folded her arms and raised an eyebrow, daring him to go on. His cowardice won…for the moment.

"I just wanted to say, thank you for this," he said, showing her that he was wearing her gift.

She softened briefly. "That goes both ways. I loved what you gave me. I didn't think it was appropriate to wear to a recording session though."

They were both relieved that they were able to laugh, even if only for a second. But the wall in Joe's mind was still high, so he chose to stay his course.

"Listen, about last night…"

"It shouldn't have happened," Maggie said, cutting him off. Better for her to administer the initial blow - she found that it hurt less that way. "It was a huge mistake. I mean, what were we thinking?"

"Mag, I don't know what's happening with me," he said. "I do know you mean the world to me…"

"But…"

"That's just it; I don't know how to fill in that blank. I mean, I think I do. When I'm by myself, I can come up with six ways till Sunday why we shouldn't get involved. Why I'm not ready to take that step. But then I see you…"

"Maggie, we need to get going in five minutes," Darla called from the main door of the studio.

"Okay," she replied.

She returned her attention back to Joe. He picked up where he left off.

"Then I see you…and it's like…everything just goes out the window." He leaned in closer to her just as her perfume wafted his way.

"I understand," Maggie breathed.

Joe shoved his hands in the pockets of his jeans. He was afraid that if he touched her, even put his fingertips against hers, it would all be over with no going back. He continued to speak from his fear.

"I just don't wanna hold you back, Maggie."

"Hold me back? How would you…"

"You've got so much ahead of you. I know that this is just a stepping stone for you. You should be with someone who can help you celebrate who you are and what you do so well…"

Maggie was genuinely confused. "Joe, what are you talking about?"

"You're young. You're on the road. You need someone with whom you've got more in common." He pointed in the direction of the building. "What about that guy you were talking to a few minutes ago? Jake?"

It took Maggie a few seconds but then it dawned on her. "No, Jared. What about him?"

"Yeah, Jared. He's good looking; you guys are in the same profession…"

Maggie held up her hand to stop him. Hold up!" she said. Shaking her head as if that action will help her make sense of what Joe was insinuating, she asked once again, "Jared?

"I saw the two of you talking, it looked fairly intimate…"

"*Jared*?!"

"Yeah, I think we covered that…"

"Joe, I…I…don't know how to even respond to that. Do you really think…"

Maggie scoffed again as Joe attempted to protest. "Do I think what, Maggie?"

"I have to go, Joe. Merry Christmas."

"No!" He grabbed her hand. "Do I think what?"

Maggie wanted to walk away. In truth, she wanted to run. But she wasn't going to let him off the hook with a simple dramatic exit. She turned to face him.

"Joe, *really consider* what you've just implied...in light of what happened last night."

His face softened with immediate understanding. How could he have been so shallow to believe that Maggie would connect with him so passionately in one moment, only to offer her affection to someone else not even twenty-four hours later? He knew that he was merely cultivating excuses for not getting close to her. He felt embarrassed and childish.

Just then, Darla came to the car. "Maggie," she said. "We should get going."

The tension between Maggie and Joe was obvious, forcing Darla to waste no time in getting behind the wheel and closing the door to offer them a final few seconds of privacy.

"Maggie," Joe finally said. "I'm sorry. Really, I am."

Maggie then said something that she would regret for the rest of her days. Her eyes narrowed as she hissed: "You're right Joe. From where I stand, you're about as sorry as it gets."

His hurt was visible immediately. Maggie turned away and got into the car. She couldn't believe how quickly she lashed out, simply to wound him. It was something Richard would have done and it disgusted her.

As he had done in his driveway just one night before, Joe stood in the parking lot and watched helplessly as another car took Maggie away.

Jared jogged over to Joe, a look of disappointment on

his face. "Oh man, did Maggie just leave?"

"Um, yeah," Joe said with a heavy heart. Jared motioned to a tall, sturdy woman with a deep complexion. She had a quiet beauty and uncomplicated sense of dress.

"Dang," said Jared. "My fiancée just showed up, and I wanted her to meet Maggie."

Joe blinked and recovered from his daydreamed state. "Fiancée?"

Jared glowed as the woman joined him and took his hand. "Yeah, Maggie's gonna sing at our wedding in the spring, and we're gonna take her out to dinner when she gets back so we can go over the songs, and thank her in advance."

"She's singing at your wedding," he said, stunned.

"Uh huh," replied Jared. "I was hoping to catch her before she went to the airport so they could at least meet ahead of time. I'm sorry; I've forgotten your name. Joe, was it?"

"Yes, I'm Joe."

"Well Joe, meet the love of my life, Diana."

"Diana, like the huntress," Joe replied, extending his hand. Diana gracefully offered hers as they shook.

"Exactly," she said with a bright smile. "I hunted this one down for sure!"

Joe hid his embarrassment by laughing along with the couple. Completely floored, Joe set his gaze in the direction of the car and sighed. "Well," he said as he fumbled with his car keys, "It was great meeting both of you."

"You too," Jared responded. "I don't know how long you've been friends with her, but Maggie has been like a big sister to me since I moved here three years ago. She heard me sing at a showcase, and kinda took me under her wing. Got me connected with some cool friends of hers.

Now I'm getting ready to sign my own deal. She even co wrote a couple of songs with me. Didn't charge a thing. She's amazing, isn't she?"

Joe found it difficult to breathe; it was as if someone has set a boulder on his chest. Somehow, he managed to say, "Amazing doesn't even begin to cover it."

At the stoplight, Darla paused before turning left off of Broadway to slip onto Interstate 40. Maggie stared out of her window, not saying a word, fighting her tears every second of the way.

"I suppose there will be no seriously juicy details to be shared, will there," Darla said, half joking. Maggie glanced over at her briefly, yet said nothing as she searched for her ticket and ID.

"I will take that as a no," Darla said.

As she pulled up to the curb side check in, Darla helped Maggie with her bags and the two of them said their goodbyes. She decided to keep her promise to Joe, saying nothing about him surprising her when she returned on the 26th, but made plans to be waiting for Maggie at Baggage Claim, just in case.

Chapter 5

C hristmas morning found Joe Buchanan rising before the rest of his family. The Hammonds were down from Ohio, sleeping peacefully in the master bedroom; his mother was given Gwen's room, while Sissy and the children camped out on the top floor in the bonus room.

Having fixed a pot of coffee and a healthy fire in the den, Joe took his place at one end of the sofa and sipped thoughtfully. The last time he sat there, Maggie was a mere three feet away, laughing with him, encouraging him, allowing him to be there for her. Joe remembered the song she sang and played that night - a musical picture he was certain she'd painted especially for him.

The sweetness of that moment, however, was obliterated by the memory of their last conversation. Joe shuddered at the thought of it all as he took another sip of coffee.

Undoubtedly, Maggie brought the hammer down hard, but Joe knew he deserved it. He'd been a fool that day. He realized that whatever his feelings for her, there was no excuse legitimate enough to deny that fact. He'd have to find a way to win back her trust; they'd been friends for far too long. Surely something could be salvaged from this mess.

Joe's thoughts were broken by the sound of softly

shuffling footsteps, forcing his vision of Maggie into thin air.

Elise was making her way to the couch, carrying her own mug of coffee. Tough as nails in the world of business and finance - a product of her father who served in the Greek army before immigrating to the US to begin his own successful company - Anastasia Elise Chrisagis Buchanan suffered no fools gladly.

But when it came to her family members, she was simply "Gramma B," her toughness tempered by a fierce love and loyalty. Grace always referred to her mother in law as The Lioness, protecting all within her world. There was nothing she wouldn't do to maintain the well being of her people.

She groaned as she sat down opposite her son. "I want you to know," she said in the genteel inflection she'd acquired over decades of living in the South, "that since I'm too old and tired to do it myself, I've decided to put out a contract hit on that boy of yours."

Joe shook his head and laughed. "He jumped in your bed with one of his Wrestler Federation pile driver moves, didn't he?"

"What in Heaven's name ever happened to entering an old lady's room politely, kissing her on the cheek and saying, 'Merry Christmas Gramma'?" she exclaimed. "I know you said you tried to raise that little knucklehead right, but I'm telling you, he's a terror!"

"I'm really sorry Mom. He didn't hurt you or anything, did he?"

More amused than annoyed, Elise allowed a smile to curl a corner of her mouth. "No, I'm fine. But I should milk an injury or something, just to make him feel bad. Maybe even throw in a threat to cut him out of the will again for good measure. Now, what's going on with you?"

Joe took another sip of his coffee and waxed thoughtful for a moment. "Oh I'm just sitting here thinking...reminiscing. You know, getting sentimental because it's Christmas. I'm missing Grace, that's all."

Rising from the sofa, Elise moved her delicate, 110-pound body directly between her son and the fireplace. Extending her hand, she said. "Hello there. I'm Elise Buchanan. It's nice to meet you."

Joe stared at her with a confused expression. "What are you talking about, lady?"

"I'm introducing myself, because apparently you think we've just met. That the biggest line of horse hooey I've ever heard," she said. "You think I don't know my own son?"

Joe smiled lovingly into his mother's face and brushed his hand against her cheek. In what world did he ever think he could fool this woman?

"Oh, I'm a jerk, Ma," he said finally.

"When it comes to expressing an honest, romantic emotion, most men are," she said.

Joe was astonished at her insight. "How did you know?"

"Okay, again we're back at the idea that you and I are strangers," she said. "I saw this coming as far back as Labor Day. Don't you remember?"

Joe nodded as he rolled his eyes. "Now tell me," she said. "What did you do? Because I know it wasn't Maggie. The girl couldn't hurt a fly."

"You're right. Maggie's amazing. And wonderful. The last few months, I've gone from just feeling grateful for her help in my life to something else...something really solid for her."

"And then, you chickened out, right?"

After an embarrassed chuckle, Joe said, "Worse. I pushed her away. Told her she should find someone with whom she had more in common. Someone who had a creative background and an open mind. Someone who understood the road she was on, and who she was inside and out. Someone...who might make a better fit into her family portrait." Elbows on his knees, Joe's head dropped in shame with the mention of his final sentence.

It was a rarity to catch Elise Buchanan in a moment of shock, but somehow, her son had managed to do just that.

"Please tell me you didn't say that," she said.

"Well, no," Joe admitted. "I didn't say the thing about fitting in the family portrait."

"Thank Heaven."

"No, before I got that far, the damage had already been done."

Elise looked upon her son with a mixture of pity and sadness. Joe raised his head and met her gaze as the gravity of his mistake gained greater clarity.

"Aw man," he said sadly. "I can*not* be *that guy*, Ma."

"I didn't raise you to be *that guy*, son."

"So, you're saying you don't have a problem with me dating someone outside my race?"

"Not really. More to the point, I don't have a problem with you dating *her*," Elise said. "She's a keeper. I've always considered Maggie to be family. She gives an incredible amount of love-to me, to you, to that brood of yours. In my opinion, she was always more of a sister to Grace when she was alive then that tall drink of West Coast water sleeping upstairs.

"You don't care for Sissy very much, do you?" Joe said in a low tone.

"You picked up on that, huh?"

"You're about as opaque as cellophane, old woman. But I thank you for at least being polite when she's around."

"Well, I'm sorry," Elise protested. "I try to be nice, but I can't help it. She's just so kissy-uppy, and drippy…"

Joe tried to hide his amusement at his mother's frankness. "Kissy-uppy? Drippy?" he asked.

"Her parents are fine…her dad's salt of the earth; her mom's a real peach, but the way that girl dotes and hangs on you…tries to suck up to me…it's just so obvious that she wants to get into your…"

"*Ma!*" Joe whispered loudly.

"*Life!*" she interjected. "I was gonna say *Life!*"

Joe laughed in relief. "Well, it's been good to have Sissy here in town. She's been a true savior at certain points."

"Just watch your back, son," she said. "I don't get a real genuine feeling from her."

"Yes ma'am," he responded.

Silence prevailed for the next few moments until Joe finally found the courage to reveal the final piece of the puzzle.

"I kissed her, Ma…"

"What?" Elise asked, terrified that he was referring to Sissy.

"I kissed Maggie."

Relieved, Elise turned to face her son. "Oh my," was all she could say. After a few moments' reflection, she said, "Define *kiss*…you know, on a scale of one to ten."

"Fifteen."

"Wow. That's something. Did you get to second?"

"Ma…"

"I'm sorry, I'm teasing. Okay, so…go on. Do you have a sense of what's going in her head?

Joe sighed. "That's hard to say. Last night, she high

tailed it out of here. But then when I saw her the next day at her recording session, she seemed genuinely happy to see me."

"Is this the part where you really messed it up?"

Joe's mouth pursed as he cleared his throat. "Yes, that's when things went sour."

"How did you leave it?"

"Well, I started off by saying something stupid. Then I said something else stupid. Then she basically ripped me a new one."

"Maggie told you off? I'm impressed. She's more of a pistol than I thought."

"Mother…"

Elise reached out and touched her son on the knee. "Sorry, sweetheart. I know this is hurting you. Finish what you were saying."

"The thing is, I know her - Maggie doesn't know how to be merciless. But she was that day. And even though I deserved it, what she said to me broke her heart as badly as I did."

In the tones of his voice, Elise clearly felt her son's pain. She took his hand. "Well. I will say this - maybe it was good that you two parted company for a while. Things sounded like they were snowballing emotionally. Always good to step back and reassess. I think it'll help you get the clearer picture that you need. But if you can get your act together and get your heads and your hearts on straight, what you two have already established will put you well on your way to creating something really special. Because if you ask me, every one of those attributes you described for Maggie's perfect man," she reached up and took his face in her aged hands, "sounds exactly like the beautiful boy that

I gave birth to four and a half decades ago."

"I'm 42."

"Whatever. Now can I say something that just won't leave my mind?"

"You're asking permission to express yourself? Are you feeling alright?"

"Hush up and listen to your mother," she said. "Here's what I think. There's something to be said for your apprehension over the racial differences between you and Maggie. But what's really got you up this early is the notion that you're actually considering moving on with your life. More specifically, with your love life."

Once again, Joe was astounded. He was unsure of how to respond, because he knew that, as usual, she was probably right.

"Wow," was all he could manage to say.

Elise's face took on a look of sheer pride. "I know. I'm a genius, aren't I? I really wish you'd get it through that thick, uncut mane of yours that I know everything."

Joe chuckled and grimaced at the same time as Elise continued.

"Sweet Grace has been gone for nearly two years now…and in that time, I've seen you fall apart, put it back together and give your all for the sake of your family. Maggie was there with you every step of the way, pulling you out of a pit that even I as your mother had no clue how to help you out of. And as you said, at first it was gratitude, but now it's grown into something more. Face that. Admit it to yourself. Be honest, *please*."

She moved in closer to him and took the mug of coffee from his hands and placed it behind her on the coffee table where she'd been sitting. Their knees touching, she took his hands in her own and stared him down.

"You were a precious child. You are an exceptional man. No mother could be prouder of her son. There are women in pretty much every corner of this city who know you who would give their right arm to be at your side."

"Oh, come on..." Joe protested.

"No, I'm serious. You finding another wife? That's bound to happen eventually. It just scared you that someone got caught in your crosshairs this quickly. You just got knocked off balance is all. But know this: what you have to give in the next chapter of your life takes nothing away from what you and Grace first shared."

Joe nodded. He knew if anyone understood, Elise did. In the decade-plus since his father had died, there were a number of gentlemen who would come calling on the Widow Buchanan, and while none had yet to match the power of Joseph Senior, She had never closed her mind to the possibility of sharing her life with someone again.

"I suppose I feel a sense of wanting to protect her," Joe said finally. "I'm still a little anxious that people will give her a hard time; like she was waiting in the wings or something. As if she had an underhanded motive for wanting to help so much."

"Anyone who knows that girl could never accuse her of having one ulterior bone in her body," Elise interjected. "Besides, I think there's another person right here in this house who fits that bill."

Joe's brow furrowed. "Who, Sissy?"

Elise's head swayed from side to side in disbelief. "You *seriously* do not see the designs that girl has on you?"

Joe was embarrassed at his own naïveté. "Sorry Ma. I've just never seen her that way...so I guess not."

That was enough for Elise. She knew her son had no

reason to be coy; that wasn't in his nature. "Okay," was all she said.

"So, with that in mind, what do I tell the Hammonds?"

Elise gave a soft laugh as she transferred herself from the coffee table back to the couch. Patting him gently on the knee, she said, "Let's eat this elephant one bite at a time, okay? Your first order of business is to get things straight with Maggie. Enjoy a courtship. And then figure out together what the next step should be."

"Thanks Mom. You really are one smart lady."

"I know. Glad to see you finally got the memo."

The two of them laughed.

"Hey you guys, Merry Christmas!" said a very cheery Sissy as she peeked into the room. Already wearing makeup with her hair pulled in a youthful pony tail she chimed, "What are you two up to?

"Merry Christmas, Sissy," said Joe.

A small crash, the sound of skin being slapped, and a yelp followed. "I take it the kids are up?" he added.

"Yeah, and we should probably get in there and read the Christmas story so we can dive into these presents before the twins bust a gut," she said. "Merry Christmas Gamma B!" she chirped.

"It's 'Gramma' not 'Gamma', you simple little…" Elise said under her breath through a frozen smile. Her sentence was cut short by Joe pretending to have something stuck in his throat.

Sissy furrowed her brow. "I'm sorry?" she asked, lost as to what was happening.

"I was just saying, Merry Christmas to you," Elise returned.

"Okay, I smell coffee, so I'm gonna grab a cup, and as soon as Mom and Dad come down, we'll get crackin'!" she said with the enthusiasm of a high school cheerleader.

"Great!" Elise said, forcing a smile while drawing out the word. With a quick nod of the head, Sissy bounded out of the room, stopping to goof around with the kids before turning on some lively Christmas music to coax her parents down from their slumber.

Elise stared straight ahead into the fire, noticing that the house had begun to brighten with the light of day. She sighed heavily, not looking forward to a morning in Sissy's presence.

"I suppose we can table our conversation for another time," she said as Joe rose and extended his hand to help her from her place. Placing both hands on his arms, she looked at her son and said sternly. "You've given a tremendous amount to the world around you, son. It's time to see about yourself. Now, get me one of those bibles off of the shelf, please."

"Well this is a treat, Ma, are you gonna read the Christmas story this year?"

"No child. I'll leave that to you or to Judge Matthew. Between your son and Sissy, I really believe it would be in everyone's best interest if I kept the Word of God close by. Just think of it as life insurance."

"You're a trip, Ma," Joe said as he turned to search the shelves for one of his favorite translations. Handing it to her, he paused briefly before saying, "All that stuff that happened last week with Maggie...it felt like this whole world opened up for me. When I kissed her, sure there was a physical reaction. But I think what really got me was the connection I felt with her. It was intense, Ma. Really intense."

"That my dear, is what you need to explore," Elise said, patting him on his arm. "And before you do anything else, child, pray. I like to think I have all of the answers, but I know the score. The Good Lord is the only One who truly knows what you need. He'll help keep you from letting anyone else's agenda get in the way."

"I hear you. Thanks for the advice. I love you."

"It's my pleasure, son, because I really love you."

Joe tucked her arm into the crook of his and began to lead her out of the room. "Okay, Elise," he said as they made their way to the living room to the rest of the family. "Promise me you'll behave in there."

"Disrespectful boy. Won't get a haircut, calling his mother by her first name..."

"Hey, you gave birth to me and you can't even remember how old I am."

"That was an honest slip, young man. I'm old. It happens."

"Look at it this way; you just named the only two flaws in my character."

"Oh, if that were only true."

"Ha!" he laughed. *"Kala Christougena, Mana."*

"Kala Christougena, my sweet boy."

"You know, I've always meant to tell you that your Greek sounds hilarious with that Southern accent."

"Oh, shut up."

The story of the Christ child was read reverently, as always, by Matthew, ushering in a beautiful prayer by Joe, all serving as a prelude to children doing their duty in decimating the room as they opened their gifts with delight. For the adults, watching the children's fervor, listening to them squeal - "Oh thank you! It's just what I wanted!" - was the best part of the morning's entertainment.

Once the adrenaline had run its course, there were three small bodies lying amongst the ruin of opened gifts and discarded paper, each of them napping comically while clutching their favorite gift.

Matty had somehow worked his way completely beneath the tree, curled on his side, hugging his brand new Marshmallow Shooter gun.

"Who got him that," Matthew asked.

Sissy raised her hand sheepishly. "Guilty," she said. Joe and Matthew groaned in unison.

"My only fear is what he's gonna experiment with once he runs out of marshmallows," said Joe.

"I don't know what I was thinking," said Sissy. "But what could I do? He was so cute when he kept pestering me about it, so I just couldn't say no." The looks on everyone's faces were still skeptical as to the soundness of her judgment. "Okay, okay. We'll 'conveniently' lose it later," she yielded, using her fingers to form quotation marks.

Gwen had fallen asleep sitting on the floor, resting her head on the loveseat, a brand new leather Deana Timmons World Tour jacket from Maggie spread across her lap. Mary Margaret lay spread-eagle under some paper in her footie pajamas and matching bathrobe; the newest American Girl doll in one hand, the accompanying book in the other.

"Breakfast is ready," Janice whispered.

"Should we wake the children," Sissy asked.

"*No!*" the other adults whispered emphatically.

"Just step over the bodies and enjoy the peace and quiet," Joe said as he climbed over the back of the couch.

They enjoyed the spread of freshly brewed coffee, egg casserole, smoked sausage, citrus fruit salad and homemade cinnamon rolls as the music played quietly and the children continued to sleep. Joe, sitting next to his mother, enjoyed the stories that each of the Hammonds shared from Christmases past, interjecting with memories of his own as they all laughed aloud.

"Shhh! You don't wanna wake the kids up," warned Janice.

Matthew rose and peeked around the corner. "At this point, I figure they'll sleep through Armageddon if they've slept this long," he said. As he returned to his seat, he suddenly got serious. "I want to say something. It's been a rough season for us all. But it's a real blessing from God that even though we still miss our beautiful Gracie, we can gather together in love. I'm thankful for that."

Taking Sissy's hand, he continued. "We're still here, still together and still a family."

Janice, sitting on the other side of Sissy, put her arm around her and kissed her on the cheek. "I know that I don't say this often enough, my darling girl, but I treasure you. Merry Christmas."

Sissy's heart was filled with an overwhelming sense of thankfulness as her eyes filled with tears. For many years she'd felt as though she hadn't been valued. For many years she tried to impress her parents with the accoutrements of her jet-set lifestyle; from VIP seats at concerts and awards shows to backstage passes. And while Matthew and Janice always seemed to appreciate the gifts, Sissy still felt as though she bore the rare burden of standing in the shadow of her younger sister.

During her lifetime, Grace lent beauty to the world through her art. Sissy was more adept at the business side of things. Being a mover and shaker in the board rooms of the entertainment industry was her calling, even if it wasn't considered all that life-affirming compared to Grace's legacy.

But on this day, it was gratifying for Sissy to realize what Grace had known all along: that all it took to receive her parents love was simply just...to *be*.

She returned the embrace. "I love you too, Mom. Thank you for saying that." For the next few moments, they all remained quiet, taking a moment to savor the closeness that they shared.

Wiping the tears from his eyes, Matthew said, "Alright then, before we all get arrested by the schmaltz police..." Everyone laughed as he stood and raised his water glass. "I just want to say that I believe this New Year is going to bring with it even more strength and fresh starts than we've ever had."

The declaration released something in Joe: a settled determination to make right what was wrong. And if all went according to plan, he and Maggie could ring in the New Year embarking on the grandest adventure of their lives. With confidence, he lifted his own glass and said, "Hear, hear."

He cast a sideways glance to his mother, who responded with a smile and a wink. Her smile faded, however, as she noticed Sissy sipping from her own cup of coffee, her eyes fixed confidently-and squarely-on Joe.

Chapter 6

M aggie smiled at the flight attendant as she exited the plane; it was then she realized the aircraft had docked at the far end of the terminal. Rebuking herself for wearing the black suede stiletto boots her mother had given her for Christmas, she braced herself for the long walk to baggage claim.

Her time with friends and family-particularly her father - served to sooth the wounds she'd sustained in her argument with Joe. She received much needed counsel and comfort in the words of her childhood pastor when she'd attend church with her parents. She laughed at the Christmas movies and cheered with her father at the victories of his favorite football teams. But in the quiet, unguarded moments, Maggie's sadness would rise to the surface.

As always, Lenore kept in a state of prayerful vigilance and said nothing. She simply waited to see if Maggie would open up about what might be bothering her, and was ready to listen if she did.

Maggie never said a word.

An entire week had gone by without so much as a phone call, e-mail, text or Facebook post between Maggie and Joe, leaving her to wonder what to expect upon her return. One thing she did know: she owed him a serious apology for the cutting remark she made.

It was a comfort for her to know that Darla would be waiting for her downstairs. The two women had always had a good relationship, made even stronger with Grace's death. As a 'thank you,' Maggie thought she'd treat Darla to dinner. They could swap holiday stories and make plans to shop for the big New Year's Eve gala that was being hosted by Deana Timmons' label, Star Records. She also knew that Darla would want the lowdown on what happened the night before and the day of the session, so there would be no lack for conversation. It was the least Maggie felt she could do in response to all of Darla's kindnesses.

It had been a while since Maggie had indulged in a girl's night. They just weren't the same without Grace. However, Maggie felt a need to finally move on. Not just with her social life, but with everything. There was a deeply held hope in her heart that she could move past the unpleasantness with Joe as well.

Finally reaching the escalator, Maggie made her way down to the next level to claim her bag. She was searching through her purse for her cell phone when something caused her to look up.

There, leaning against one of the large concrete pillars that stood between each conveyor belt, was Joe. Smiling broadly, he held in his left hand a bouquet of colorful flowers; and in his right, a crudely cut cardboard sign that simply read, "Maggie."

Slowly, she made her way over to him. She didn't get too close, stopping with at least a foot between them. She wanted to look serious; she wanted to be self-controlled. But her joy was unmistakable and impossible to hide. She felt as though the sides of her face were going to split from the extent of her smile.

"Okay," she said, putting a hand on her hip. "I have two questions."

"Fire away," Joe replied as charmingly as he could.

"How did you steal the job of airport shuttle from Darla?"

"Don't you think I know how to charm a pretty lady?"

"You see me smiling, don't you?"

Joe gave her a look of surprise. "Well, well - guess we can check 'self confidence' off of the list of things to get Maggie for her birthday. Apparently she's all stocked up. Alright, hot shot, what's the other question?"

Maggie closed the distance between them slightly. Pointing at the flowers, she asked, "How in the world did you find those in the middle of winter?"

"Oh, I have my *veys*," he said in a bogus German accent. She snickered as she crinkled her nose in that adorable way that always made him smile; and took the flowers from his hand. She marveled at their beauty as he continued to marvel at hers. Suddenly, she looked up at him.

"Joe," she said softly. "What I said last week before I left was inexcusable..." Joe silenced her with a hand to her lips.

"Uh uh," he responded. "As far as I'm concerned, there is nothing to forgive, except my own fear and stupidity. What I said to you was lame, Mags. I'm so sorry for everything."

Joe gathered Maggie in his arms and held her close. For the briefest of moments, he felt a flash of apprehension that people might be staring at the two of them. But he remembered the insight of his mother and banished those thoughts as quickly as they came. It felt far too wonderful to hold this particular woman in his arms without any fear of what *she* might be thinking or feeling. *Let everyone else be hanged,* he thought. Maggie West was there with him because she *wanted* to be. That was good enough for him. They could figure everything else out along the way.

For Maggie, taking in the warmth of Joe's embrace had, at last, washed away the final vestiges of all her pain, her insecurity and her doubt.

Joe pulled her face into his field of vision and began to kiss her slowly; first on each side of her face, then her nose. He chose to pause for a moment to gaze at her, studying her face before placing a kiss squarely on her lips. When they separated, she regarded him with a look of surprise at his newfound boldness.

"I don't wanna let you go, Maggie," he said in response to the questioning in her eyes. "I think we've got the chance to create something really amazing here. If you want to, that is."

Maggie's eyes became liquid with emotion as she snaked her arms around his neck. "That's the best gift you could have ever given me. Thank you, Joe."

They shared another hug and another kiss before retrieving Maggie's bag from the conveyor belt and returning to Joe's car, walking hand in hand.

The small blond woman is acting rather strangely, the airline customer service attendant thought. As the odd woman crouched within a self made fortress of unclaimed luggage wearing large black sunglasses, he figured at first she was merely hiding. Or crazy. But when she removed the glasses and pulled the binoculars from her handbag, it was clear to him that she was spying on someone...*and* crazy.

Periodically, she'd turn around and smile nervously at

the attendant, with a look that said, 'Pay no attention to the lady hiding in the stack of Samsonites.'

Darla held her post for a good ten minutes, relieved that Joe had actually arrived, and did so with flowers. Once she saw the look on Maggie's face as she came down the escalator, Darla knew all she had to do is wait on a phone call from Maggie later on. Her mission was complete.

"Yes!" The attendant heard her say.

Calmly, Darla rose from her hunkered-down position, returned the binoculars back to her handbag; and with a flourish, looped her silk scarf over her head and around her neck. The attendant stood in confused awe as Darla, adjusting her sunglasses and smoothing her clothing, exited the terminal with an elegant walk, as if what she'd just done was the most normal thing in the world.

Despite the thin, fresh blanket of snow that had fallen the day before, there was an electricity in the air of Downtown Nashville that only New Year's Eve could bring.

As was the case each year, Star Records All Star-Gala was one of the most anticipated events of the season. The mix of artists, actors, politicians and the famous-for-being-famous was a true feast for the eyes, the ears and the tabloids.

In order to fit the evenings chosen theme, The Roaring 20s, set designers were flown in from Hollywood to create elaborate art deco facades. Gangsters and gun molls served as wait staff, while security stood sentry with prop Tommy Guns along the walls. The whole affair had the look and feel of a high-class speakeasy. The stage, located at the far end of the dance floor, housed a Gershwin-esque orchestra, filling the air with the sounds of the era. It was obvious that no expense was spared.

Maggie and Darla exited their cab in front of the venue, linking arms to shield one another from the cold. Giggling like excited schoolgirls, they gave their names to a stern, heavily built man placed in charge of guarding the door. From his fedora to his spats, the man looked like he could have been an extra on the set of any gangster movie.

Catching a glimpse of herself in a window, Maggie took a moment to check and make sure that everything in her outfit was where it should be: A peacock blue silk tunic gown, with a slight ruching at the waist, draped her body. The color gave her skin a radiant glow; the sweetheart neckline gave proper shape to her full figure.

Matching, intricately beaded Christian Louboutin pumps that she found on the Internet completed her look. Her hair was ironed bone-straight and tucked behind the ear on her right side, revealing crystal and gold chandelier earrings.

"Woo hoo hoooo," Darla said, as she unveiled her curve-hugging black halter dress from beneath her coat. "I'm tellin' you what girl…we look good!"

Maggie smiled uncomfortably, as if she wasn't quite sure, but Darla would not tolerate one ounce of doubt. She stood behind Maggie and held her by the shoulders. "No, no, no. You. Look. Breathtaking," Darla said firmly, but earnestly.

"So do you, honey. I'm scared of you in that teeny-weeny dress."

"Well, this teeny-weeny dress and I need a drink," Darla cracked. "Somewhere in this room there's a martini with a gorgeous man attached to it, and they're both waiting for me."

They stepped past the sign-in area, and for the first

time, they were able to take in the whole scene.

"*Mon Dieu*," Darla whispered, her French bathed in her slow, southern drawl.

"I know…right?" said an equally awed Maggie.

After a slight glance around the room, Darla said, "Alright, Sister, you might wanna see if the gorgeous Mr. Buchanan has arrived. He will pass out when he sees you!"

Maggie and Joe had discussed the party the evening he picked her up from the airport. She was surprised that he knew about it to even broach the subject, but less surprised by his admission that Sissy had extended the invitation to him over Christmas.

Completely oblivious of the stares of admiration she was receiving, Maggie decided to make her way to one of the numerous beverage tables to get a drink and settle her nerves.

As she stood in line, she fanned herself slowly with her hand, trying to decide what it was she wanted - or rather, needed - to consume.

"Club soda, with an extra twist of lime?" said a voice from behind her. The smoothness of the sound caused Maggie's blood to run cold. She turned around with very little enthusiasm.

"Happy New Year, Richard," she said, her face never changing expression.

"Happy New Year, Maggie. How've you been?"

"You aren't blind, you tell me," she said, holding her arms out in order to give him the full picture.

His pride made it difficult to admit, but Richard was impressed. "If you're living as fine as you're looking, Baby Girl, then you're doing quite alright."

"You look…exactly the same," Maggie said cautiously. She didn't want to give him too much room.

"Thanks, I think," he said with a slight chuckle. He turned his attention to a well endowed, twenty-something blonde. She was dressed beguilingly in a pink-on-black pinstriped vest that revealed her toned midriff, matching pants, and a pink necktie that seemed rather unfortunately trapped in her cleavage. "The lady will have a club soda, extra lime. I'll have a Crown Royal."

Richard paused for a moment to admire the young bartender before returning his attention to an unimpressed Maggie. Handing her the soda, he simultaneously sipped his drink, wincing at the taste of it.

"Ugh," he choked. "Guess they're trying to stretch the booze out by watering it down. Cheapskates."

"You know, you can always leave, if what they have isn't up to your standards," Maggie said. "What, by the way, *are* you doing here?"

"You sure do like asking that question."

"Well, I wouldn't have to ask so much if you didn't keep showing up."

Richard laughed. "Oh yeah, that's right. I remember you got some spunk somewhere down the line. That's cool. I ain't mad at ya," he said haughtily. "But since you asked, this particular invite came from the president of the label. Your father had nothing to do with it."

"Good for you," she said as she tried to turn away. She lifted the crystal tumbler in his direction. "Thanks for the drink."

"Guess it's my version of a peace offering."

Maggie rolled her eyes. "Look, Richard, I don't wanna talk about that. It's water under the bridge as far as I'm concerned. I've moved on." An awkward silence passed between the two of them before she said, "Look, I've gotta go."

Richard reached out to take hold of her hand. "What, are you trying to leave?"

"Yes dear, she's got better ways to waste her time," Darla said practically out of nowhere as she grabbed Maggie's other arm.

"Darla...always a pleasure to see you," Richard said, eying her lasciviously,

"Richard...Always fun being ogled by you," Darla returned. "Okay Killer, time to go," she cracked as she whisked Maggie away.

"Try and have fun without me, Richard," Maggie yelled over her shoulder. "I'll make sure to leave you some dessert!"

"Maggie! You are bad," Darla exclaimed as the two women disappeared laughing into the crowd.

Richard remained cool as he sipped his drink. His irritation over her bravado made him want to knock Maggie down a peg or two. He cared less about her personal growth than he did about his own personal vindication. He returned his interest to the blonde behind the bar.

"What's your name, sugar," he asked.

"Brooke", she said in a rich alto that immediately captured his attention. "Brooke with an 'e'."

"Well, Brooke with an 'e', if you don't mind, I'd like another please. And um…" He leaned against the edge of the bar without dropping his gaze for a second. "Make it stiff…okay?" As he stared the mesmerized barmaid in the eye, he increased the wattage of his smile and upped his game. "If you don't mind," he said.

Returning his flirtation with a smile that indicated that

he could get lucky if he phoned the number she'd placed on his drink napkin, the pretty blonde handed him his second drink. "Enjoy your evening sir," she said sweetly. "Come back...*anytime.*"

Richard lingered on her confident sexuality for a number of seconds before turning his gaze back toward an exuberant Maggie. Now he was truly aggravated. What right did she have to be happy? She was the hick town, loser bar singer he picked up and polished up and made presentable to Nashville.

At least that's how he chose to see it.

And she was gonna leave *him*?

A low grunt escaped his throat as the downed the second drink and straightened his tie.

No one disrespected Richard Davidson.

No one.

"Oh that felt so good! Thanks for the assist," Maggie shouted over the din.

Stopping in her tracks, she spotted a man who, from the back, looked like Joe.

"I do believe, that's what you came for, Darla said," pointing in his direction just past Maggie.

Upon closer inspection, although she couldn't see his face, Maggie could tell that it was most certainly Joe Buchanan. She took a few steps forward, suddenly halting as if someone had placed a barrier in her path. Darla ran to her side.

"What's up, Maggie?"

Both ladies saw it at the same time; a pair of delicate hands draped over his shoulders. But before their hearts could take a tandem nosedive, they both began to laugh.

The hands belonged to none other than his eldest daughter, Gwen. As she came into view, she caught sight of Maggie and immediately ran to her.

"Aunt Maggie, I am so excited to see you…I can't tell you how excited I am to be here…you won't believe all the people I've met already…its just all been so, like, exciting! And Aunt Sissy promises that tonight I'll get to hang with Deana Timmons!"

Her entire sentence came out in one breath, causing Maggie to laugh out loud.

"Sounds…um…*exciting*," said Darla, a bit taken aback.

She's so very much her mother's child, Maggie thought before saying aloud, "Hey, kiddo - breathe! Sounds like you're having a really good time."

Her efforts to focus on Gwen's enthusiasm were thwarted, however, at the sight of Joe's approach. Joe was never a fan of the tuxedo, despite his love of quality clothes. But his choice for the evening was nothing short of impeccable: A black single-breasted suit, a crisp white shirt and a blue tie that was perhaps one or two shades lighter than Maggie's dress.

"Maggie," he said. "Words fail me. You're gorgeous…no, more than gorgeous. You're…"

"You too," was all Maggie was able to say.

"Maggie, it's so good to see you," a cheery voice cut through the din. "You look fantastic! Is that new?

There was Sissy, a vision in white Dolce and Gabbana; her hair expensively styled in a configuration that would make any sculptor proud, accented with a cluster of gardenias on the side.

"Hi Sissy, thanks. You look like a goddess yourself," she said.

Sissy struck a pose. "Well, I like to think so," she said

as she looked at Joe and winked.

Again, Joe found himself bewildered by Sissy's attempt at flirtation. His conversation with his mother flashed quickly through his mind, producing a kind, albeit somewhat impersonal smile. "You do look nice," he said.

"Thanks Joe," she said; her tone somewhat breathless with humility and appreciation.

Turning her attention to her niece, Sissy asked a still wide-eyed Gwen, "Are you ready to talk music with your hero?" Sissy pointed to a table toward the back where Deana and Charles sat sipping cocktails, surrounded by what one could only assume were an assortment of industry-types, all styled and coiffed within an inch of their lives.

"Seems Gwen and Deana hit it off at the big Christmas party," Sissy said proudly. Placing her arm around Gwen, she bent down to meet the child's field of vision. "They're practically BFF's now," Sissy cooed as Gwen giggled.

"BFF's...*wow*," Darla mouthed to Maggie, forcing her and Joe to stifle a chuckle. Darla quickly turned her attention to a handsome, significantly younger man at a drink station. Maggie got the gist that that was where Darla preferred to be, and waved her off.

"Maggie, why don't you join us?" Sissy said, her arm still gesturing toward the table.

"Why? I talk shop with those two all of the time," she said sarcastically.

Sissy gave a slight roll of her eyes. "Not them, silly girl..." She pointed to a woman seated just to the right of the Timmonses; the true focus of the group's conversation. "Her."

The woman in question had an elegant ease about her: Lustrous ebony curls were piled atop her head in a way that seemed messy and organized all at the same time. The jet-black velvet of her gown, with its plunging back, coupled with her hair to bring a richness to her alabaster skin. Long fingers softly cradled a glass of white wine, which swayed ever so slightly as she gestured.

"Who is that, Aunt Maggie?" asked Gwen.

"Oh wow…that's…" Maggie began.

"Lanie Hoyos," said Sissy, guiding them toward the group.

"Who's that?" asked Gwen.

"She's kind of the boss of all of us," Sissy said. "Definitely my boss, that's for sure. And Maggie…I think it's time she met you."

Regardless of the perceived altruism, Sissy's motives were anything but. Her primary purpose was to guide Maggie in any direction away from Joe Buchannan. In her heart of hearts, Maggie was aware; but she chose to keep her mind focused on the situation in front of her.

"Lanie," Sissy cooed, greeting her boss with air kisses. "You look absolutely amazing. Happy New Year!"

"Well, Gwen Hammond," Lanie replied in a soft, husky voice that might have indicated one too many cigarettes in her younger days. "Happy New Year to you as well. Ha!" she teased, pushing Sissy out to arm's length to regard her outfit. "Don't we look like polar opposites tonight. Am I the bad guy and you the good?"

Sissy laughed, but chose not to directly respond. "Oh Lane, you're such a card," she said instead. "Listen, I want to introduce you to a friend of mine…"

"Maggie West," Lanie said, cutting in. She half-folded her arms, propping the elbow of the one that held her wine on top of the other. "No introductions are necessary.

Charles and Deana and I were just chatting about you. Were your ears burning?"

Maggie's smile exuded genuine warmth. "Lanie, it's really an honor," she said. Reaching her arm around little Gwen, she began to introduce her. "I want you to meet..."

"Oh, this is my niece, and my namesake, Gwen," Sissy abruptly interrupted, swooping in between Maggie and Gwen. "Gwennie, this is a very important person in my work life, Ms. Hoyos."

"Hi," young Gwen said brightly.

"Hi yourself," said Lanie.

"I have to tell you, Gwennie has an *amazing* voice," Sissy said. Maggie simply gazed at her with a fixed smile, wondering when Sissy had ever actually had the opportunity to hear the child sing. The look on the child's face expressed similar surprise; a moment not lost on Lanie. Few things were lost on Lanie Hoyos.

"Ah," Lanie said. "Isn't that nice? Who knows what might happen for you tonight, Little Miss," she said benevolently, cupping Gwen's chin in her hands; the rich red of her fingernails grazing the child's cheek. "I've always said Nashville is an enchanted town...dreams tend to come true here more powerfully than anyplace else it seems." Gwen's face glowed with excitement.

"Well...far be it for me to let any more time pass between the meeting of the two most talented women in this town," Sissy broke in. "Gwennie darling, let's go see what Charles and Deena are up to. Maggie...Lanie...I'll just leave you to it, 'kay?"

"Yes," Lanie purred, "Why don't you? Miss Gwen...it was a pleasure."

"Nice to meet you too," Gwen replied, practically

curtseying. "See ya later Aunt Maggie."

"Bye, sweet girl."

As Sissy whisked her young charge away, Maggie returned her attention to Lanie. Her gaze never leaving Maggie's face, Lanie simply extended her left hand. As if on cue, the tanned and toned Brooke with an 'e' appeared with two glasses of white wine.

With a sweet, somewhat mysterious smile, Lanie merely tilted her head in Brooke's direction. "Chardonnay?"

"Sauvignon Blanc," the young woman replied.

"Better," Lanie stated, extending her arm to hold out her old glass. A sweet-faced twenty-something brunette wearing a rather sad but earnest blue taffeta gown stepped up and took the lukewarm wine away while simultaneously pushing her dark glasses up along the bridge of her nose.

"Thank you Beth," Lanie said. Taking the fresh glasses in hand, she immediately passed one to Maggie. "I know that there will be champagne later, but I would like to propose a toast now."

Maggie was still somewhat overwhelmed by the command this woman seemed to exude. She knew Lanie Hoyos only by reputation, and what she knew was daunting. Her years of being in a relationship with Richard Davidson however, had trained Maggie in creating a professionally effective poker face.

"Okay," Maggie said cautiously. "To what are we toasting? The fact that we've got a better wine?"

Lanie's ability to laugh without moving one solitary muscle on her face led Maggie to wonder just how in demand that woman's plastic surgeon truly was. "I would like to propose a toast to what I believe is the discovery of one of the greatest voices this industry will ever know," Lanie said. Raising an eyebrow, she continued. "And to the maverick genius that's going to make sure the whole world gets to hear it."

Unaware of how confused her expression had become, Maggie was unnerved when Lanie took her arm and led her to a more secluded spot to speak. Deana had been pleasantly occupied by her conversation with Gwen and Sissy; Charles, however, was completely distracted.

"Charles," Deana said maintaining a smile through clenched teeth. "Please let us not break our necks spying on Maggie and Lanie Hoyos, okay? I'm sure they're just having a little friendly girl-talk."

"Right," Charles replied, finally turning his attention back to his wife. Sipping his drink, he repeated, "Right."

Lanie offered Maggie one of two plush seats at a small table by the wall. The lighting was intimate, and they were able to more comfortably converse away from the insanity and music of the party. "I'm sorry, my dear, I didn't mean to alarm you," Lanie said. "But your name has been tossed about for quite some time in the halls of my LA office."

Maggie's face registered genuine surprise. "Really," she asked.

Lanie gave another expressionless laugh. "Please accept my apology for not approaching you sooner, but yes, *really.*"

Maggie gave a bemused shake of her head as Lanie continued.

"Now, I realize I'm known for bringing my office with me wherever I go..." Lanie began. As Lanie's fingers splayed in that stylish fashion employed by spokesmodels revealing what's behind curtain number three, Beth seemingly materialized from thin air and reappeared at her side.

"Maggie, meet my...*office*. This is Beth. Beth, this is Maggie."

"Nice to meet you," the two women said simultaneously. Pushing her glasses back up the bridge of her nose, Beth handed Maggie a card. Artfully printed on impressive stock was Lanie's information. She gave Beth a kind wink, which essentially cued the young woman to scuttle back to whatever alternate dimension from which she'd emerged.

"Obviously, this is not the place to do any in-depth dealings," Lanie said. "That's my personal cell and the address of the apartment I use whenever I'm in town. I loathe hotels," she sighed with a far-away look and sipped her wine.

Maggie inspected the card. She recognized the approximate location of the address; surmising that if you're Lanie Hoyos and you loathe hotels, of course you're going to rent a penthouse apartment in The Gulch.

Lanie toyed with an errant curl, casually winding it around her finger as she silently regarded Maggie. "I'd like to speak with you first of next week after the holidays," she continued. "Lunch. Tuesday. Noon-thirty."

It had the tone of a request, Maggie thought; but something told her that if she had plans with anyone or anything less exalted than God Himself, she would have to cancel them.

"I was on the schedule to perform brain surgery, but I think we can put that on hold till Wednesday."

Finally, the corner of Lanie's crimson lip curled into a smile. "I knew I was going to like you," she said. "Glad we connected, darling. See you Tuesday."

Again, Maggie continued her internal monologue; *dismiss the tone...this is not a request.* "I look forward to it," she said aloud.

"Well, that's a look of undeniable joy," Joe said as Maggie made her way toward him. Placing his glass of punch on the table, he took Maggie's hand in his and twirled her around. "Dance with me and tell me all about it," he said.

As he led her to the dance floor, Maggie felt as though she were floating above the crowd. "Oh Joe, I've gotta tell you...I really wasn't looking forward to this party..."

Joe pretended to be offended. He backed away and held out his arms. "So are you telling me I put all this together for nothing? What a waste!"

"Okay, let me try again," Maggie said, working her way back to his arms. "You...*and* the last fifteen minutes were the only real reasons I'm glad I came."

"Now that's more like it. So...what was the deal with ol' Maleficent over there?"

Maggie laughed. "I kinda think of her more as the long lost, long-legged member of the Corleone family."

"Okay, I'm officially scared."

She laughed again. "That's the label's Senior Vice President, Elaine Hoyos."

"She sounds important."

"She is. And she wants to meet with me on Tuesday."

"Is she gonna make an offer you can't refuse?"

"Judging from the way she's talking, I don't think I wanna refuse."

Joe raised an eyebrow. "Well, you gotta make sure you give me the lowdown once it happens. Do you think she's gonna make you an artist?"

"I dunno. From the way she tells it, she's a huge fan…"

"Of yours? Seriously?"

"I know!"

"Who-da thunk it?"

"That's what *I'm* sayin…"

The two of them reveled in their silliness. "Anyway," she continued. "I'm curious to hear her game plan. And you will be the first person I call when it's done."

"Maggie," Joe said, drawing her in closely. "I am so incredibly proud of you. I think this very well might be your moment, sweet lady."

And for the first time in her life…Maggie agreed.

Joe twirled Maggie again and again until she lost her balance and fell into his arms. As he gathered her up, the two of them engaged in exaggerated dance moves, laughing and taking in the moment.

Nursing his fourth drink, Richard fiddled with the napkin Brooke had given him. He managed to distract himself for the better part of the evening shaking hands and networking; dropping Maggie's name whenever he thought it might serve his interests. But as Gwen made her way to Maggie and Joe, it turned Richard's stomach to see the three of them acting like a family.

He refolded the napkin and stuffed it in the breast pocket of his jacket. Brooke could wait. In his extensive experience, women like Brooke always waited.

Suddenly, the music died down and a jovial voice permeated the festivities. Following an obnoxious series of taps on and subsequent feedback from the microphone, Duncan Wilder, president of Star Records took control of the program. "Ladies and Gentlemen," he said in a booming tenor. "Everybody having a good time?"

The question was met with resounding, somewhat

drunken cheers. "Okay, for those of you who have been enjoying the evening a bit too much, I wanna remind you that there's a shuttle service to make sure the streets stay safe later tonight. For those of you who are still upright without the aid of the wall, the chairs, or anyone around you..."

Laughter emitted from the crowd, followed by a loud whoop from someone at a far corner of the room. "Unlike that guy..." More laughter. "Don't forget to thank the toilet bowl for being cool on the side, brother!" The laughter was now widespread. Wilder held up his hands to calm the crowd. "Okay, so it looks like we're about 5 minutes away from a new year..."

The crowd cheered as he signaled to the wait staff to begin distributing glasses of champagne. As he gave instructions, Gwen tried to coax her dad into letting her having one glass. "Not on your life," he kept saying, despite her protests.

As the clock wound down, Maggie secured a glass of ginger ale in a flute for Gwen, who accepted it begrudgingly. "Cheer up" she said, enveloping the younger girl in a hug. "At least it looks the same." The two laughed.

As the countdown grew closer, Richard strode across the room, making a b-line for Maggie. Sissy arrived with her glass and zeroed in on Joe. Squeezing her way in between the two of them, she put her arms around both their shoulders. "Happy New year!" she said joyfully. Turning to Maggie, she said, "Make sure you don't leave without your New Year's kiss. It's bad luck not to!"

My having a year's worth of bad luck would probably suit you just fine, Maggie thought.

Uncomfortable with Sissy's proximity, not to mention the pushing of the crowd around him, Joe managed to maneuver himself over by his daughter, and turned his focus to the platform, where a giant digital clock was counting down the time on a large screen.

"Two minutes to midnight!" Wilder shouted. The frenzy of the crowd was near fever pitch at this point. Richard passed by Darla, who had been enjoying her evening with the object of her attention.

"Oh my giddy aunt," she said out loud as she saw where he was headed. She jumped up from her stool in an attempt to get Maggie's attention; her diminutive frame, however, kept her from being seen. Leaving her bewildered suitor by the bar, Darla worked her way through the crowd as quickly as she could, ducking and weaving past people along the way.

"Thirty seconds!"

Joe reached over to his daughter and gave her a hug. "Happy New Year, my darling daughter."

"Happy New Year, Dad."

The crush of the crowd pushed Gwen into her father, and the two of them away from Maggie. As Joe and Gwen laughed at the absurdity of it all, Darla found herself within arm's reach of Maggie.

Joe and Maggie locked eyes, realizing that the prospect a New Year's kiss for them was a lost cause. "Sorry," she mouthed. She smiled and crinkled her nose as she always did in uncomfortable moments. He returned her apology with a smile; a smile that quickly turned to an expression of alarm as he saw Richard approaching.

Richard circled his grip around Maggie's wrist just before Darla was able to intervene.

"Ten seconds!" Wilder shouted over the roar of the crowd.

Richard whipped Maggie around and pulled her in, their noses practically touching.

"Nine...eight...seven..."

Confetti and balloons prematurely began to fall from their netted places in the ceiling. "Five...four...three...two...one..."

"I'm gonna get my due," Richard said to a terrified Maggie.

"What the...? Richard, no!" Maggie yelled. Her protest was swallowed up by the cheering of the crowd.

"Happy New Year!" the whole room said in unison.

Music blasted from the orchestra. Richard's lips barely brushed against Maggie's as she managed to break and turn away. A silver platter fell to the floor as Maggie collided with waiter carrying a tray of hors d'oeuvres.

Caviar, smoked salmon and cream cheese blanketed the fabric of Maggie's dress. While practically unnoticed by the party at large, those within a few feet of the calamity witnessed the spectacle.

Richard backed away; the nature of the moment made more comical by his inebriated state. "Guess you don't have to worry about having a second helping of *anything* now, do ya?" he taunted.

His laughter, however, only brought out a deep anger in Maggie. As Joe shielded his daughter from the drama with a bear hug, Maggie shook off the food from her arms and regarded her ex-boyfriend with a primal sense of disgust.

"How old *are* you, you stupid jerk?" she shrieked. Richard placed a hand to his ear, his expression signaling that he heard nothing she said, despite the fact that he heard every word. He spread his arms and asked, "What's your problem?"

Maggie knew that the appropriate reaction would be to walk away. But she knew she had to end this. She approached Richard slowly and carefully. Taking his hand in hers, she smiled…and used her opposite hand to punch him in the face.

"*You* are my problem!" Maggie shouted as Richard fell to the floor. Surprised by her own prowess, Maggie didn't falter. She approached a bewildered Richard with a bravery that was otherworldly. Bending down, pieces of food dripped from her gown onto his suit. She didn't care. Nose to nose, she shouted. "Correction. You *were* my problem. But if you *ever* come near me again…"

Too disgusted to finish the sentence, Maggie realized she'd made her point. Astonished onlookers backed up to give her clearance; several witnesses actually applauded her.

Still hugging Gwen, Joe motioned to Sissy. "Help me get my daughter out of here," he said sharply.

"But Joe, she's fine. Maggie and Richard have obviously had too much to drink," Sissy countered.

"Daddy?" Gwen asked, attempting to turn around.

Joe's reassuring smile hid his worry. He took his daughter's face in his hands. "It's late, sweet pea. Time for Cinderella to leave the ball. Stroke of midnight, remember?" Looking back at Sissy, who was divided between what was in front of her and Maggie sending Richard to the floor, Joe implored, "Please Sis, take Gwen home."

As Sissy whisked Gwen away, the child turned, barely missing a humiliated Richard, hand on his bloodied nose, being led to the nearest men's room by his nursemaid, Brooke with an 'e'.

"Aunt Maggie?" Gwen called.

"Aunt Maggie will see you tomorrow, sweet pea, she's um…got a little something on her dress and needs to get it off," Joe said as he helped usher her away.

Maggie was equal parts humiliated and empowered. Catching Joe's eye however, she had no idea what to make of the expression on his face.

Darla finally made her way over to Maggie. "Okay sister," Darla said., "let's get you outta here." Tears bubbling over her lashes, Maggie looked up at her with a helpless expression and allowed her friend to get her out of the building.

"Don't worry sugar," Darla said as she assisted Maggie into a waiting cab, "I don't think anyone of any real importance saw what went down."

Not exactly true, Maggie thought to herself.

Chapter 7

The dress was probably ruined, but Maggie chose to soak it in cold water anyway. She stood over the sink, staring, but not really focusing on what was in front of her. The pain in her hand had subsided to a dull throbbing. Holding it in the water eased the physical discomfort, but her hand was definitely the last thing on her mind.

Somewhere between the agony of her embarrassment and the ecstasy of her time with Joe, Maggie wondered where the events of the evening had left things between the two of them. It didn't help that nearly an hour had passed and she had yet to hear from him.

She changed into a comfy set of loungewear she bought for one of the longer trips on the tour bus with Deana. Well worn but not worn out, it was Maggie's favorite thing in which to relax. But relaxation would not come easily. She needed some assistance.

A fire in the fireplace, a mug of her favorite Earl Grey, and the one millionth showing of *The Philadelphia Story* from her DVD would soon set Maggie to rights. *Tomorrow will take care of itself,* she thought. In a couple of days, she'd meet with Lanie, and finally set the wheels of her career in motion.

"Happy New Year," she said aloud as she raised her

mug in a mock toast. Shutting off the lights, she curled up and did her best to dissolve into the world of Tracy Lord and C.K. Dexter Haven.

The spell of the movie was abruptly broken by a knock at Maggie's front door. Jumping nearly a foot off of the couch, she wrapped her afghan around her and made a slow approach. Her first thought was that it might be Richard. He was a master of retaliation. But then she remembered Brooke with an 'e'. The thought of the young, eager blonde playing nursemaid to his wounded nose as well as his ego put Maggie's mind at ease. She laughed off the fear and figured he would be fine.

Looking through the peep hole, her fear dissipated at the sight of Joe loosening his tie on the other side. Pausing to turn on the light, she collected her excitement before letting him in.

"How you doing, slugger?" he asked playfully as he walked through the door.

"Don't mess with me. The feeling's just about back in my hand," she said. The smile in her eyes betrayed the lack of levity in her voice.

Joe moved closer to her, his smile that familiar look of warmth and comfort. He placed his hands on her shrouded arms, and began to rub them up and down. He was in awe of how precious and young she looked with her freshly scrubbed face; her hair in an innocent ponytail.

"You look good," he said dreamily.

"So do you," Maggie said.

"You okay?"

Maggie cast her gaze to the floor and nodded. Her embarrassment returned, and she found it nearly impossible to raise her head. Tears sprang fresh from her eyes as she placed her injured hand over her face.

"Hey, hey now, come on," Joe said softly. "No tears. You did nothing wrong."

Scoffing, Maggie took a step backward out of his grasp. "Joe, I totally humiliated myself!" she cried. "I saw your face. You were disgusted by the whole thing."

Joe moved in to close the gap between them. "I was disgusted by *him*, Maggie. He was obviously drunk and disrespecting you. Besides," he began, his face taking on a somber appearance as he straightened his posture for emphasis. "I would have cleaned his clock myself, you know, if I didn't have to worry about getting Gwennie outta there."

Maggie's expression turned from pained to amused. "*Cleaned his clock?*"

"Oh come on. You know what I mean."

Maggie co-opted an East Coast accent. "What is this, New Year's Nineteen *Eighty Five*, Mr. Buttafuco?"

Joe's machismo melted in the light of her mockery. "You know what? You are a horrible little person," he said.

Maggie continued her teasing. "I'm sure Richard wouldn't have stood a chance squaring off with you, mister-big-tough-buddy-boy."

"You are just mean!" Joe laughed. "For the record, as lit as he was, I at least had that in my favor." The two continued to laugh as he began to take her in his arms again. "Okay, I am being serious now," he said. "You can obviously take care of yourself. I'm proud of you. I really don't think he's gonna mess with you anymore."

"Man, I hope not."

"You taught me a very important thing tonight, you know."

"Do tell."

"Next time I get in a bar fight, I'm callin' you for backup."

Maggie pushed him away, pretending to be offended.

"That's it...time for you to go."

"Nuh uh," Joe said, looking in the direction of the television. "Not when I see you're watching *The Philadelphia Story.*"

Maggie knew the hour was late and that Joe's due diligence was complete. He'd checked on her and saw that she was fine. Reassurances were made. The two of them were fine. There was no real reason for him to stay. But she wasn't ready for him to leave just yet.

"You gonna be comfortable watching a movie in that?" Maggie said, regarding his suit.

Joe was momentarily dissuaded before his memory was suddenly jogged. He snapped his fingers. "Mom gave me some clean laundry when I took the twins to stay with her," he said. "It's still in the trunk of my car. And before you say anything, yes, sometimes my mother does our laundry. Well, actually, her housekeeper does."

Maggie shook her head in disbelief. She was already caving in. "Bathroom's upstairs," Maggie said, resigned. "I'll fix some popcorn if you're game?"

"Perfect," Joe said enthusiastically.

Maggie walked into the kitchen, still chiding herself for conceding so readily. Placing a pan on the stove, she suddenly stopped. Without the afghan around her, she was quickly reminded that while her loungewear was more than appropriate, the fact that she wore nothing underneath was not.

"Whoops," she said. "Big girl...no bra...that's not happening."

She ran to the laundry room to see if there might be one in the dryer. Thankfully, there was. She donned it quickly and awkwardly before returning to the kitchen.

Standing in Maggie's immaculately plush bathroom,

Joe found the tones of lavender and pale gold alluring; the design of the curtains, the walk-in linen closet, the vanity and stool all revealed a woman's touch without being, as young Gwen might term it, "too girly." He picked up one of the clear, delicate bottles of perfume that sat on a small gold corner shelf on the counter. Relishing the sharpness of the sandalwood fragrance, he could tell that this was the scent she loved most. Closing his eyes, it was if she were standing right in front of him.

Maggie knocked on the door. Joe opened it, wearing only the sweatpants. He had his T-shirt in one hand, preparing to put it on.

Maggie was speechless. The sight of this man, who was, despite nearing the mid point of his forties, in particularly good shape, practically made her knees buckle underneath her. Dark brown hair, with flecks of gold and grey made perfect wavelike patterns across the olive tones of his chest and stomach.

Not knowing what she might be thinking, but hoping it was something good, Joe's posture straightened, the slight paunch in his stomach drawing in ever so slightly.

The adolescent nervous laughter returned for both of them. "Hey, was just about to call down for some hangers for the suit," he said. "What did you need?"

Maggie looked confused. "What?"

"You knocked. What did you need?" He couldn't suppress his smile, knowing he was making her nervous.

"Oh yeah, right. I was just going to tell you where the linens were, if you needed them," she said. "Um...the uh, hangers?" she pointed to a door behind her. "There should be some good ones in there."

"Okay, Thanks."

"And I was gonna go pop some popcorn for your

chest...I mean...the movie, so um...I'll just...meet you downstairs."

"Wait a minute."

Joe stepped out into the hallway. He leaned against a wall and folded his arms.

Okay, please put that t shirt on right now, or I'm gonna have a friggin' heart attack, screamed her mind.

"Come here," he said. He was tired of waiting. He wanted her in his arms at that very moment.

"What?" she asked, trying to sound as though she were in control.

"Come here," he said slowly. His tone was commanding. Dark. Incredibly sexy. The sound pulled her in, and she didn't try to fight. He took her face in his hands, and she placed her hands lightly on his forearms.

As it was the first time, there was a slow dance between their lips as the kiss began. But this time, there was no self-consciousness, no guilt. They took their time in finding their perfect fit; and once they did, they found themselves back at the edge of that jagged cliff, preparing to fall into the fantastic unknown.

Joe's arms went from her face to her hips as he engulfed her completely. Maggie wrapped her arms around Joe's neck, the feel of her chest against his sending her into total delirium.

His kisses moved from her mouth down to her neck, sending a shower of sparks from the top of her head to the soles of her feet. She could feel herself slipping away, willing her feet to the bedroom that was a mere three yards away.

She was just about to give in when Joe placed his hand on a wall to brace himself, inadvertently knocking down a framed picture behind Maggie's head.

Maggie used the time it took to retrieve the fallen photo to gather her wits and strengthen her resolve. "Looks like it's okay," she said of the photo. Examining it closely, she returned it to its place on the wall. Still facing the wall, she closed her eyes and drew in a breath. She exhaled and turned to face him.

"Joe…"

"I know, I know. Too much."

"No," she said breathlessly. "Not too much. Just too fast. Now, I'm going to make the popcorn, and *please*, for the love of God….*put that shirt on.*"

Maggie placed a tray with a large bowl full of freshly popped corn and two matching tumblers full of soda on the coffee table. "*The Philadelphia Story* has got to be one of the best classic films ever" she said.

"Couldn't agree with you more. Great call, West."

"Glad you like it, because you don't get a say. My house, my rules."

"You are a cold-hearted woman. Quit hogging the popcorn, pass the bowl."

Maggie hesitated, pretending to offer the bowl, quickly jerking it out of his reach. His reflexes proved to be faster as he finally caught it.

"Dude, you're spilling it!" she laughed.

"Stop whining, watch the movie," he replied.

In a rare moment of assertiveness, Maggie grabbed Joe's hand and looped it around her shoulders. The move caught him pleasantly off guard. He paused for a moment and kissed her on her forehead as he drew her more securely to his side.

Chapter 8

From the moment she left the party, Sissy's mind was in overdrive. In truth, she did feel a slight twinge of pity for Maggie's dress getting smeared, but she wanted to kick herself for leaving without Joe. *It wasn't that big of a tragedy, after all.*

The call she made to him around 1:30 that morning was more of a means to check on his whereabouts, but she'd already purposed within herself that she would pretend to care about Maggie's state of mind. When his phone eventually went to voice mail, her paranoia soared through the roof. She managed to keep her emotions under wraps however, as she helped Gwen get settled in for the night.

When Sissy woke the next morning, a small stain of disappointment was already beginning to spread in her spirit. The first thing she did was check to see if Joe had returned her call. There was nothing displayed but a series of congratulatory text messages from colleagues, lauding her efforts on a successful party.

Gazing out into the gray and silver tones of the cold January morning, she hugged a large, down-filled pillow to her chest and let out a small groan. She wasn't sure which was frustrating her more: not knowing exactly what was happening between Maggie and Joe, or the fact that she allowing this fixation to eclipse her own professional triumph. In all her life, she had never been one to allow her feelings for a man to derail her in this fashion.

But Joe was just too good to let slip away, and while in the back of her mind she knew her desire for her brother-in-law seemed a bit sordid on some level, she still felt as though she were the only person worthy of his affection; almost as if she was destined to be Grace's heir apparent.

What was it about Maggie West that was so important to Joe? And why couldn't he see that woman was absolutely and completely wrong for him?

The evening's events merely proved her case: Maggie and that boyfriend of hers seemed to generate drama wherever they went. Not just last night, but that whole thing at Thanksgiving. As far as Sissy was concerned, Maggie and Richard should just go off and leave her family in peace. They deserved one another.

Her thoughts raced as she turned on her side in her bed and gripped the pillow even harder. *Joe wouldn't dare debase himself with someone so common. He wouldn't do that to Grace. He wouldn't do that to his kids. He wouldn't do that to....*

The fabric of her chiffon dressing gown flowing gently behind her, Sissy rose and made her way down the hallway to her guest bedroom. The morning light came through the window, heightening the brilliance of the all white furnishings.

Sissy loved the clean, uncomplicated nature of white. She saw it as a blank canvas on which she could create any visual she desired. White empowered her...be it clothing, décor...or skin color.

A smile came to her face as she walked over to the bed. Gwen was still sleeping peacefully in a room she'd come to adore. She always felt so grown up whenever she got to hang out with her Aunt Sissy...the finest clothes, restaurants, parties. Her own bedroom with her own private bath was her favorite part of the stay.

The meticulously custom designed bathroom had the feel of an island bungalow. Shutters on the windows and silk foliage all around lent to the tropical air. Faux marble steps led up to a sunken bathtub large enough for at least three people, complete with Jacuzzi jets and an oversized bath pillow against the side. Thin, gauzy material hung from the ceiling above the tub like a canopy.

Gwen would light practically every candle in the room, put on some music, and luxuriate as though she were a European princess. She never needed to pack a bag, as Sissy always had some fabulous new pajama set, and something for her to wear the next day.

The twins were always welcome, but they preferred to stay with their grandmother, who had among other things, a life-sized play house where the two children would often invite their friends for full-day play dates.

For Sissy, however, it was all well and good. She loved doting on her eldest niece. But she knew that eventually, if her plans were ever to come to fruition, she'd need to gain the love of all three children, not just Gwen.

If she could just eliminate that fly in the ointment...Maggie West.

Sissy tilted her head to the side, and stroked Gwen's hair. She made a decision to try and call Joe again.

It's 7:30, she reasoned internally. *Surely he's up by now.*

Chapter 9

Sissy was right. Joe was awake. But he was much too occupied with the fact that he'd been able to simply hold Maggie for an entire night. At one point, he got up to get a blanket to cover them, bringing them even closer together. Maggie had, at another point in the night, shifted her position so that they were lying face to face, still wrapped up in one another.

And this is how Joe awoke; to the smell of her hair as her head rested on his chest and arm, to the warmth of her body as she snuggled against him like a small child. If he could have, he would have chosen to never move from that spot again.

Maggie made a soft little sound as she began to stir. Instinctively, Joe kissed her on her forehead.

"Morning," she said, her speech muffed by his chest

Joe laughed. "Good morning. How you doin,' kiddo?"

Hand over her mouth, Maggie looked up with sleepy eyes and said, "Aside from what I know is ferocious morning breath, I'm pretty good, thanks. You?"

Joe's head tilted back in laughter at her silliness. Pulling her hand away he said softly, "I'm good."

They shared one of the sweetest, most decadent kisses that either one of them would ever know. It was then and there that Maggie decided her favorite time of the day to be kissed would be at dawn's early light; no pretense, no artifice. Just real, raw life, brought together by the beauty of genuine affection.

"Wow," she said, when their lips finally parted, "You are amazing. I love…"

The two of them froze for a moment as those tiny words escaped Maggie's heart.

"I…I mean, I love that you got this great blanket," she stammered. "That was awfully thoughtful of you. She tried to get up from the couch casually, but nearly stumbled over the coffee table.

Joe tried not to laugh, and Maggie pretended not to notice. "I'm gonna need some coffee, I think," she said. "As you can see, I can't function well without it. You want some?"

Joe rested his head on one hand and gave her a skeptical smile. "Sure. Coffee sounds great," he said.

He looked impossibly handsome in that moment, his hair mussed just perfectly in that Hollywood leading man in the morning kind of way. "Great," she returned, just a tiny bit too cheerfully. "I'll get some on right now."

Out of Joe's line of sight, Maggie rolled her eyes at herself. *Idiot!* She thought. "Don't understand why you didn't just put *all* your cards on the table, Maggie…" she muttered under her breath.

Hoping she'd not done too much damage, she began fixing the coffee quietly.

While part of him thought the whole thing was sweet, there was another part inside Joe that was actually happy that she didn't complete her sentence. They were, in fact, the right words…this just wasn't the time. He knew if there were any declarations to be made, they would come in a moment that wasn't fueled by emotions and passion. It would be at a point where it was least expected and certainly not influenced, bidden or coerced by circumstance.

It would happen organically…and the timing would be appropriate.

Maggie was curious as to whom Joe could be speaking at such an early hour. She was reaching for mugs for the coffee when she realized he was in conversation.

"No, I'm sorry," he said as Maggie put the mug on a coaster in front of him. He leaned over and gave her a soft kiss and mouthed the words "thank you" as she curled up in a corner and watched him.

It occurred to Maggie that it might be Sissy, calling to check up on him.

"Well, she looked like she'd recovered alright. Yes, I went to check in on her after I got you and Gwennie out of that party. I felt better ending my day after knowing she was okay." He looked over at Maggie and shrugged. It wasn't the whole truth, but it wasn't exactly lying. Maggie just shook her head, smiling, while continuing to drink her coffee.

"Oh, that's good," Sissy said, as she paced her living room. "I guess I got a little worried when you didn't call. I figured you'd let me know how she was doing after you saw her."

"Sis, you've got her number, you could have called her yourself," Joe said, giving Maggie an exasperated expression that said the last thing he really wanted to be doing at that moment was explaining his whereabouts to Sissy.

"Yes, you're right," Sissy said. "I'm just glad she's fine."

"Was there another reason you called, Sissy?" Joe asked in an impatient tone that caught her off guard. He quickly softened. "I mean, you mentioned you tried to phone me. Is Gwen okay?"

Sissy let out strange, fluttery laugh. "Of course she is! In fact, the reason I was catching you this early was to see if you wanted to grab the twins from your mother's and go get some breakfast. I think the Pancake Pantry's actually open today even though it's New Years. The kids love it there."

Joe made a sucking sound with his teeth, "Oooh, that sounds tempting, but I've got some things I've gotta do in the office Second semester's just a week away, you know."

"Well, darn,' Sissy said, truly dejected. "And to think, I was gonna invite Maggie too. I know the kids would love to see her."

"Again, you can feel free to give her a call," Joe said as he winked at Maggie. Maggie's face took on a quizzical look as Joe continued. "When I talked to her last night, she didn't mention that she had any plans; and you're right, I'm sure she would *love* to join you."

Maggie's eyes opened wide to Joe as if to say, *"How dare you?"* She stuck out her tongue at him and shook her head in disapproval, while he did everything he could not to laugh out loud.

"Uh huh, yep, uh huh, sure, Sis," he said, desperately trying to end the conversation. "I promise I'll give you a call. And thanks so much for taking all three of the rug rats today. You didn't have to do that, but I'm glad you are…you're kindness never ceases to amaze me."

"And I shall never cease desiring to be kind," she replied daintily.

"Okay, yes…well, um, I'll speak with you later this

evening," he said, now thoroughly uncomfortable.

"Sorry to have troubled you so early, Joe. We'll speak later. Bye"

"Bye, Sis."

Joe ended the call and stared out into space for a moment. "You know, I'm beginning to wonder if my mother wasn't right about her," he said thoughtfully.

"What, that Sissy's got it bad for you?" Maggie asked.

"You think so too?"

Maggie gave him a look of disbelief and laughed out loud, "Ya think?" was all she could say.

Joe frowned. "You know what? I don't think I wanna talk about Gwen Hammond any longer."

"Alrighty then. What do you want to do?"

Joe took a sip of his coffee before putting the mug on the table. He leaned over, and began rubbing Maggie's feet softly. "What I *want* to do…ain't gonna happen," he said. "At least not this morning. What I *have* to do, is look like a dork once I put my dress shoes back on with these sweats and head home. I do have to get to the office and churn out some stuff today. I hope you don't mind that I need to leave in a minute."

Maggie gave him a loving smile. "Nah, I think I'll survive. Seriously, though, I really appreciate your being here. Thank you for everything you did, and *didn't* do for me."

"You're welcome. Now," he said has he pulled her closer to him, "I'd like to kiss you one more time before I go, if that's alright."

"I dunno," she teased. "Oh, alright, if you must."

As he pressed his lips to hers, Maggie wondered if she would ever get tired of embracing this man. She decided to save that thought for another day.

✠

Joe stood at the door with his suit over his arm, looking as comical as he predicted with his dress shoes poking out from under his sweat pants.

"Oh, just go to the office like that," Maggie said with mock seriousness. "I see a whole new fashion trend starting."

"Yeah, I didn't think that plan all the way through. I'll call you later?"

"I look forward to it."

Joe stopped before walking out the door. "I just want you to know - last night was really important to me, Maggie. I don't know what Sissy's thinking. She might just be playing the role of family protector out of some sort of loyalty to Grace. But whatever the case may be, as far as you and I are concerned - I like where this seems to be headed. I really do."

Maggie stood in the center of the room, hugging herself, partly from the cold coming through the open door, but mostly because Joe's words sent a rush through her soul so intense that she feared she'd pass out from sheer elation.

"I like where this seems to be headed too," she said softly.

There it was again: that innocent expression, that soft, girlish voice. It was too much for Joe to stand. He dropped his suit and met her in the middle of the room, enfolding her in his arms, never wanting to let her go.

Leaning back just enough to take in her face, he was touched by the fact that Maggie's eyes were wet with emotion.

"Joy?" he asked. "Please tell me I'm looking at joy."

"Joy," was all she could say as a tear bubbled over and spilled down one cheek.

One final kiss and another goodbye then Joe reluctantly pried himself away and returned to the doorway. He pointed at her and smiled. "I am definitely calling you later," he said.

Maggie's countenance was radiant as she softly said, "You'd better."

Chapter 10

M aggie hid her nervousness as she entered Lanie's apartment. As she handed Beth her coat, she heard a gentle humming from her cell, signaling that some sort of message had come in for her.

"Can I interest you in a mineral water," Beth asked, pushing up her glasses yet again.

Recalling the mineral water she drank during her ill-fated meeting with Deana and Charles, Maggie began to politely decline as Beth said brightly, "Or, we have some coffee. How does that sound?"

"Coffee sounds great. Cream and sweetener?"

"Coming up."

With Beth gone and Lanie yet to arrive, Maggie chose that moment to sneak a look at her text:

How's it goin'? Remember, you're already a star-Call me later. Xoxo J.

Smiling as she returned the phone to her purse, Maggie decided to take in her surroundings. Sleek, sophisticated and silver was the theme: The walls, the accents, the light fixtures. Everything was silver with little pops of color throughout.

"Of course, the kitchen's stainless steel," she breathed with a small laugh. A two-sided fireplace provided a division between the living and dining areas. Floor to ceiling windows not only offered a more than adequate amount of natural light, they also offered one of the most spectacular views of the Nashville skyline she had ever seen. As she marveled at how an apartment could actually have a staircase leading to another floor, Maggie could music - *her* music - coming from a room up there.

"Ms. Hoyos will be down momentarily," said Beth, from somewhere behind her. Maggie put her hand to her chest, closed her eyes and swallowed hard. *That girl needs a bell or a theme song or something*, she thought. She turned to face the small brunette with the kind smile, coffee cup on saucer in hand. Maggie took the cup, thanked Beth and followed her into the living area.

Just then, the doorbell rang. "Excuse me," Beth said.

Maggie had no idea that anyone else was going to be taking part in this meeting. As she heard muffled conversation down the hallway, her attention was directed to the top of the stairs, where Lanie was preparing to descend.

It was the simplest of outfits - jeans and a plain white long sleeved shirt - but somehow Lanie gave it style. Perhaps it was her mane of glossy, coal black curls, still, all over the place, and at the same time perfectly ordered. Perhaps it was her makeup - barely there and perfectly applied. Perhaps it was the fact that she didn't so much walk as she glided. No, it was almost as if she *floated* on some sort of ethereal plane. Maggie fought every urge within herself to want to be this waif-thin vision of austere beauty.

With a look of thoughtful contemplation, Lanie slowly made her way toward Maggie. "Well then," she said. "I have just one question for you, Maggie West."

Another pause.

"Where have you been all of my life?"

Maggie blinked as the question took shape in her mind. Lanie gave her a sly wink, and Maggie realized that a joke was being made, and the two women laughed aloud.

Through her laughter, a sound of sheer relief escaped Maggie's throat. "You really like it?" she asked.

"Sweetie, let me tell you, this is some of the most refreshing material I've heard in a while. I think we could do something revolutionary with this stuff."

"What did you have in mind?"

"Look, I realize that we live in an age where we're always worshipping youth," Lanie said, tossing her hair back with one hand as she strolled further into the living area. "Ugh, my colorist and my dermatologist would be first in line to tell you stories."

*Come on...*Maggie thought. *'Fess up to the botox...'fess up to the botox...*

Moving on from her internal opinion, Maggie confessed aloud, "Well, to be honest, I've been told that my music's too...um," she paused for a moment before continuing. "I've been told that *I'm* too old to be trying something like this. That's why I've always been a bit hesitant to play my stuff for anyone."

"That's exactly what I'm talking about" Lanie broke in excitedly. "We're gonna get your age, your experience, your reputation and that magnificent voice, to work *for* you. I'll get your music directly to a more mature audience."

"You can do that?"

"Of course I can. Let the other labels look for the next fetus to sign on the dotted line. Your music is for grownups, pure and simple."

Maggie felt herself once again hurled back in time; suddenly seated at the piano at her parents' home. Floating through the intricate chord progressions, Maggie sang one of her very first songs for Grace; who sat silently on the couch, eyes closed, drinking in the sound.

The final strains of the song hung in mid air, and Grace remained silent, as if savoring the final bites of a sumptuous meal. At a rare loss for words, Grace simply let out a low sound of approval from her throat. "*Stunning,* Mag. Just...stunning." Her eyes were wet with emotion. "It's the kind of song that only the person who lived life could really understand, ya know?" Grace said softly. "It's like...music...for grownups..."

"...do you know what I mean, Maggie? Maggie?" Lanie snapped her fingers to jar Maggie back to the present.

"Oh wow, I'm so sorry...I was just trying to take all this in. What were you saying?"

"Baby Boomers," Lanie said. "I'm talking about Baby Boomers. They're getting hip to the technology, to social media, and they are creating a rather unique opportunity, 'cause they've got the cash to spend. So even though what we're planning is a sizeable risk, I have every confidence in you. You are a sure bet, Maggie West. Your voice is absolute money. I honestly can't believe you've not been picked up and utterly exploited sooner."

Maggie chuckled at Lanie's candor. "Well, I think I have been, but..."

"I'm sorry, I don't follow," Lanie said, confused.

Pushing the recollection of her conversation with

Deana and Charles from her mind, Maggie smiled sweetly. "Never mind. Anyway, you're totally making my day with this."

"You're welcome. Ah, our third party has finally arrived. Now we can get things going..."

"Sorry I'm late, darlings. Hello, Maggie."

"Sis...um, I mean, Gwen. Hi..."

With her usual brusqueness, Sissy swept into the room, tucking away her cell at the conclusion of a phone call on which she'd been when she arrived. "I'm so sorry. I've been about 30 minutes behind all day. But I didn't want to miss out on being in on the ground floor of something this special. So, bring me up to speed."

Annoyed by Sissy's hyperactivity, Lanie turned her attention back to Maggie. "Gwyneth and I have been going over a strategy to get you out there, and as soon as she cools her jets, we'll lay it out for you," she explained in a slow, pointed tone.

Realizing her faux pas, Sissy blushed.

"Again, I'm sorry. I suppose I'm just excited."

"Indeed," said Lanie. She motioned for Sissy to take a seat.

Lanie chose a lux club chair on the north end of the marble coffee table; the other ladies positioned themselves in opposing seats on either side and faced her. After stretching her arms to the ceiling and taking in a deep breath, she exhaled; folding one long leg over the other, her eyes still shut. For Sissy and Maggie, it was prolonged, awkward silence. But for Lanie, this was how her battle plans came to fruition.

The cool reserve of Elaine Hoyos was undeniably her trademark. Preferring contemplation to conversation, she'd honed that reserve early on; surviving the egomania and chauvinism of her peers along the journey.

In the beginning, for a very brief period, her beauty kept her from being taken seriously. The covers of glossy magazines and the catwalks of Europe were, for some, the ultimate goal. For Lanie, they were stepping stones that guided her all the way to a Wharton MBA.

In her second year as an assistant to the Director of Accounting at a fledgling label called Star Records, she used her silent powers of keen observation to become the architect of what would turn out to be a multi-million dollar acquisition of two mainstream labels and three independent imprints to raise Star to the ranks of the majors...inking the deal three days before her 35th birthday.

Always on her own terms, Lanie was a power player's power player who single-handedly ushered Star into its golden age, where bands and artists of every stripe and genre made it their aspiration to make Star their musical home.

Maggie loved her immediately. Her tough exterior/soft interior reminded her of Joe's mother Elise; someone who took no prisoners, and suffered no fools. And just like Elise, once you had earned her loyalty, a more formidable ally could not be found.

Beth surreptitiously arrived once again with more coffee, notes for the meeting and paperwork that needed attention.

"Thank you Beth, dear."

"Can I get you anything else, Ms. Hoyos?"

"I'm sure you'll think about it before I do, darling," Lanie said. "But we're good for now. Let us know when lunch has arrived."

"Absolutely," Beth said with her usual unadorned

pleasantness. "I took the liberty of speaking with the chef at Watermark. They will be here in about half an hour with your usual favorites."

"Genius as always," Lanie said.

"Anything else?" Beth asked.

Lanie wrinkled her nose and gave a slight shake of her head. During one of the few times Beth was actually seen making her exit, Lanie leaned in and said to the other two women, "She's the daughter of one of my dearest friends from college. Loves the business, is completely devoted to me." She sipped her coffee as she stole a glance to see if the girl was nearby.

"She is absolutely indispensable...always two or three seconds ahead of me. But I've gotta get that sweet thing a bell or something. Sometimes she scares the crap outta me with those silent entrances of hers. If I didn't love her like a daughter she'd totally creep me out."

Lanie's admission nearly made Maggie laugh out loud. She wanted to reveal her similar assessment, but chose to keep her mouth shut. She sipped her own coffee silently as Lanie dove into her game plan.

The three chatted amiably about song selection, photo shoots, stylists and plans for a star-studded showcase. By the time their lunch had ended, a clear direction and goal had, to Maggie's amazement, been mapped out.

"I just love it when the women get together," Lanie said as they walked to the foyer of the apartment. "We know how to take care of business in just over hour!"

"Ladies, I cannot tell you how much I am looking forward to this," Maggie said as she donned her coat. "And you," she said to Sissy. "It's so cool that you'd want to help me out like this."

Sissy's smile was slow, and to Maggie's way of

thinking, slightly more solicitous than necessary. "Well, there's no denying your talent, Maggie," she said, the silken nature of her voice confirming Maggie's suspicion with chilling accuracy. Sissy walked over to Maggie and slipped an arm around her shoulders. "And, as I've said on more than one occasion…you're like family."

It was an oft repeated sentiment from Sissy, and until that very moment, Maggie could never understand why it always felt more like disingenuous sarcasm than a compliment. But it finally dawned on her: It was that small word that created a separation: "You're *like* family."

It was a backhanded affirmation that said no matter how warm and accepting the Hammonds and the Buchanans might be toward Maggie, she was not truly one of them. And as far as Sissy was concerned, never would be.

It didn't matter that Sissy had spent the past decade and a half living 2,500 miles away, forging her own existence; leaving her baby sister to cultivate a bond with her classmate and next door neighbor. Sissy was a Hammond. Maggie was merely a welcomed guest.

While Maggie would have once simply cowered and hid under such a revelation, she was in no mood to buy into it on this day. There was too much good that was ready to unfold for her in her life and career. She chose to look past it all.

Maggie had artfully managed to untangle herself from Sissy's grip and gently took her hand. "Yes, I know," was all she said.

None of this was lost on Lanie, who was watching with mounting curiosity.

"Okay, girls, time to get these wheels in motion," Lanie finally said. "Maggie, I'll call you when I've nailed down

Blake Fabian to produce," she said. "I know he's gonna know the right players to get, and he'll really take your sound to the next level."

Maggie shook her head in amazement. "I still can't believe Fabian's even a possibility."

Smoothing out her amazing hair again, Lanie said, "In our world, Sweetie, *everything*'s a possibility. Leave it to the star makers. It's what we do! Now, go call whoever it is that's been texting you and share the good news."

Maggie looked at her phone and then looked at Sissy. "It's just Joe," Maggie said. "I'll call him back in a minute."

"No, no, honey, call him now," Sissy said, barely masking her jealousy. "We're done. Like Lanie said, once the details get hammered out, we'll be in touch."

"Alright then," Maggie said excitedly. Backing toward door, she stopped, momentarily dropped her gaze and said with gratefulness, "Thanks again, and I'll be waiting to hear from you. Sissy, I'll see you soon right?"

"Yes, you will," Sissy said. "Guess there's some family get-together this weekend at Joe's place." She casually flipped through the touch screen on her cell as she spoke. Without looking up, Sissy said rather haughtily, "I'm sure he'll tell you about it."

With that statement, not to mention the tone in which it was delivered, came the irrefutable truth: The battle lines had been clearly drawn. Lanie's curiosity was beyond piqued as she paused from signing some papers Beth had handed her to watch the subtle showdown.

"Actually, I got a call from him this morning," Maggie said coolly, confidently aware of the advantage she possessed. "Your parents are in town and we're all getting together after church on Sunday, right? I'm bringing my chicken pot pie."

Sissy's eyes narrowed; completely betraying the seemingly friendly smile that emanated from her lips. "Oh that sounds fantastic. But then again, you've always known your way around a kitchen now, haven't you?

With an uncomfortable laugh Maggie simply replied, "Right. Okay then, I'm gonna head out. Lanie…again, it was a pleasure. Beth, as usual, when I knew you were in the room, you were a delight."

Beth covered her mouth to hide a slight giggle as Maggie made her exit. Lanie approached Sissy, who was attempting to make another call.

"What…was…*that?*" Lanie asked.

"I have no idea to what you're referring, Lanie," Sissy replied, lowering her phone.

"So, are you gonna tell me the truth of why you pestered me to stay on this project, or am I going to use that strange little exchange to divine it for myself?"

"Lanie, I have absolutely no idea what you're talking…"

"Spare me the snow job, Gwyneth," Lanie said as she regarded her own image in a mirror. Using her fingers to comb through her hair, she said, "There's something going on between you and Maggie, and I'd be willing to bet my Jag it involves that guy. I have no intention of getting into the middle of your melodrama."

"I assure you, Lanie, there is no drama."

Lanie raised her hand, her fingertips meeting her thumb as she said, "Shut it." She raised a perfectly sculpted eyebrow to emphasize her point. "I've been in this game long enough to see when someone's playing 'keep your friends close and your rivals closer.'"

Sissy was silent as she stared off into the distance.

"Well, your nothing says everything, as far as I'm

concerned," said Lanie. She stepped in front of Sissy and faced her squarely. "I don't know what is really on your mind, but I'm telling you right now, it had better be about the music. Keep the personal stuff on the back burner. This isn't Junior High. *Capice?*"

Sissy returned her steely stare. She didn't flinch or blink. "I hear you loud and clear."

Chapter 11

"Terrific, Maggie. We've got that one down. Just terrific."

Maggie was in heaven. Lanie wasted no time in setting up everything that Maggie could possibly need for the process of putting her first project together. She had no idea what it was costing, but she didn't care. From the arrangements to the production, to the amount of creative freedom Blake Fabian was allowing her to have, Maggie was willing to sell just about everything she had in order to afford it.

In the month she spent working side by side with one of the hottest producers on both coasts and every major market in between, Maggie and Blake were becoming a well-oiled machine. There was hardly a move that she wanted to make that he'd not considered a split second before. With every single song, they knew they were creating sheer magic.

Her only regret was that her musical journey was taking her far from Joe. He would visit the studio from time to time, but with the semester at the university hitting its own stride, they stole whatever time they could with brief lunches, the occasional dinner date and late night phone calls.

Blake pressed the button on the console that allowed

him to communicate inside the recording booth. With a smooth Australian baritone he said into the microphone, "Okay, Maggie, we've got one more tune to work out, and then we're pretty much done for the day. How ya feelin'?"

Maggie sat contentedly on a stool, still basking in the glow of her efforts. "I'm almost sad to see it end," she said, stifling a yawn.

"You need a break?"

She looked at her watch. In ten minutes it would be eleven p.m. If she could get the last song done reasonably well in the next hour, she could catch Joe before he headed to bed. But she didn't want to rush the final song. It was the one that she, Lanie and Blake all agreed had the strength to be the first single. Recording had gone well. The players did their job superlatively, laying down instrumental tracks in record time with-pin point precision. With all of that efficiency, there was time to slow down, and Maggie decided that she wanted to take advantage of it.

"You know what, Blake? I think I'm about done for the day. Any chance we can close it up for the night?"

Blake rose from his chair and took a sip of tepid coffee. Wincing as he swallowed, he pushed the button on the console again. "Hey, you don't have to ask me twice. I'm beat."

Maggie gathered her things and returned to the control room to hear Blake giving instructions to the engineer and two technical assistants. "How's noon sound for you, luv?" Blake said, as Maggie entered the room.

"Noon's fine. Thanks."

Blake gave her a warm smile as she made her way over to him. Tall, lanky and ruggedly handsome, his thick blonde hair was perfectly mussed with the intended just-out-of-bed look. He leaned on the edge of the mixing board, casually crossing one leg over the other. With a flash of his greenish-blue eyes, he said, "Maggie West, this has truly been one of the greatest times I've had in studio in quite some time." He then took her hand and kissed it.

She felt her cheeks flush as she uttered a simple "Aw, thanks. It's been a thrill working with you too, Blake."

"Listen, it's still early by Nashville standards. I was hoping to wind down with a drink over at Tin Roof. Care to join me?

Perhaps it was the combination of the accent, the eyes and the whimsical hair, but if Maggie didn't know any better, she could have sworn that Fabian had been flirting with her from the moment he'd arrived in town. Not long ago, she might have actually considered his invitation. But her attention was elsewhere these days.

Still, the man was flat out gorgeous, and she was sincerely flattered.

My goodness, she thought, *when it rains, it pours.*

She said, "Mmm, that's tempting; it's been so long since I've just been out. Can I take a rain check?"

Still holding her hand, he bowed slightly and squeezed before finally letting it go. If there was one thing Blake Fabian could sense, it was when a woman's heart was not voluntarily up for grabs. *Ah, but there's still a little more time before the project's completed,* he thought. *There will be other opportunities.*

For the moment, he decided to relent. "Already spoken for, eh?" he asked.

"Yeeeaaah," she said, drawing out the word lightheartedly.

With a wink and a turn he said cheekily, "Well, if it doesn't work out…"

Her confidence in full bloom, she swayed her hips in

an exaggerated fashion as she sauntered toward the door. "Oh honey, you couldn't handle it," she joked, drawing laughter from Blake and the other guys in the room. "G'night!" she said cheerfully

"G'night," all of the men said at various times.

"I'm pretty sure I could handle it," Blake said to the guys, who acknowledged their agreements with raised eyebrows and lowered grunts. "God knows I'd have a good time tryin'."

Maggie smiled to herself as she exited the building. Scrolling down her phone to Joe's number, she couldn't imagine how life could get any sweeter.

She looked at the clock. It was a few minutes past eleven. Joe was usually still awake; but even if he were in bed, he always welcomed a wakeup call from her, so she took her chances and pressed the button.

Sissy placed the neatly folded dish towel over a stainless steel rack. Locking the dishwasher door and pressing a button, the low purr of the first soaking cycle began as she turned out all of the lights in the kitchen, save the one over the stove. Its solitary glow cast a warmth over Joe's freshly cleaned kitchen. She stood in the doorway that led to the living room and admired her work. As was always the case when she'd spent the better part of a day there, she indulged herself in feeling as though this were her home.

She'd spent the evening helping the kids with

homework, making them dinner and lovingly seeing them off to bed. With Sissy taking care of the children, Joe was able to work with minimal interruption, for which he was certainly grateful. There was a *bit* of self-sacrifice in her deed; she knew that Joe needed to work, and she was much less expensive for him than a sitter. But her true satisfaction came from achieving her primary purpose: using the music to keep Maggie as preoccupied as possible; thus keeping her away from Joe.

Finally emerging from his study, Joe simultaneously walked and stretched before collapsing on the living room sofa next to Sissy. "Thanks so much, Sis," he said through a yawn. He reached over without thinking, grabbed Sissy's hand and kissed it. "You have no idea how much you've saved me today."

Sissy felt the rush of his touch from her fingers to a point somewhere in the depth of her stomach, and took advantage of his fatigue by gently maintaining a grip on his hand. "It was my pleasure, dear," she said.

With his free hand, he scratched his head and made a low, tense sound. "Ugh," he sighed. "I am so wiped."

Staring at his profile as he sat motionless with his eyes closed, Sissy allowed her mind to travel to that place where it was the two of them at the end of a long hard day, sharing stories of his activities at the university; hers at the record label. In her perfect world, they would sit on the couch and share their dreams and hopes for the children.

They were fantasies she indulged for years, practically from the moment they met. She'd long since gotten past the guilt she felt where Grace was concerned.

She tried to think of a topic, any topic that would keep the two of them engaged in conversation. "I can only imagine. You've been really burning the candle at all ends this week," she said. "How's it all going over there at the school?"

Joe finally withdrew his hand and leaned forward, bemused by Sissy's interest in what he did for a living. Glancing over his shoulder, he gave her a warm smile. "It's not without its daily dose of drama, but all in all, it's a good semester, thanks for asking." Turning to face her he asked, "You've been pretty busy yourself, Ms. Executive producer. How's that working out?

It was a subject she was hoping they'd never broach, but the inevitability was just too great. "How's what going? You mean Maggie's project?"

"Any other amazing vocalists we know in common?"

With a manufactured smile, Sissy worked to remain upbeat. She rose from the couch and made her way back to the kitchen, hoping that by busying herself she could mask her disinterest in yet another discussion about the greatness of Maggie West.

Calling out to him as she poured a glass of wine, Sissy said with faux brightness, "Oh, She's kicking butt out there. She's focused, brilliant, wowing the socks off of all of us. I've never seen anything like it." It galled Sissy to admit to herself that her comments weren't just for Joe's appeasement. She was telling the truth.

As she returned with a glass of chilled Pino Grigio in each hand, she said in her sophisticated tone, "What I can't understand is why she'd make *you* stay away. You're missing some really incredible moments."

With an irritated expression, he leaned back and stared at her directly. "What? She's never made me stay away. Why would you say that, Sis," he asked.

Sissy realized she was letting her confidence run a bit too far ahead of her. Quickly backpedaling, she said, "I'm sorry; I've just never seen you there. I figured it was safe to assume…"

Joe softened his attitude. He was tired, easily irritable and missed Maggie incredibly. Feuding with his sister-in-law was not a way he wanted to expend his energy. With a much more even manner, he said, "I'm usually there to catch the tail end of something she might be doing; between my schedule and hers, we don't get much time to hang out. But yeah, I'm there."

"Well, then, you know a little of how well it's going," she said as she sipped her wine.

"I do have one question, though."

"Shoot."

"Every time I'm there, there's always that big Marlboro Man-type guy who seems to have the whole room spellbound. The one with the accent. Who is that guy?"

Sissy closed her eyes and sipped again, taking a moment to relish the fortuitous situation in which she now found herself. "That's Blake Fabian, producer extraordinaire," she said.

"Where's he from? Australia?" Joe asked, his expression clouding over.

Sissy could sense his concern. She proceeded cautiously. "Yep. I've known Blake for years," she went on, "And I have to admit, on the one hand, he's one of the best in the business. On the other, the man *is* a charmer. I can't think of one woman on the planet who hasn't been blindsided by that accent."

Joe stared straight ahead and made a low sound in his throat that clearly conveyed disapproval.

He is jealous! Sissy thought. She motioned to the wine; Joe merely pursed his lips and shook his head. "You read the magazines much," she asked.

"Never been a tabloid kind of guy, I'm afraid," he replied.

"Well, there was that little pop star he managed to romance right out from underneath the clutches of her A-list actor fiancée," she said with a smirk. "Three weeks before the wedding, as a matter of fact. Blake Fabian knows women as well as he recognizes how to craft a hit, that's for sure."

"I'm sure it was more than his voice that reeled her in," Joe said ruefully.

Embracing her slight upper hand, Sissy ran her fingers through her hair and said, "I know how focused Maggie is, but I'd be shocked if she's not as caught up in his hype as any other girl he encounters. But then again, she's a pro. She won't let anything stand in the way." Another sip of wine, she felt her confidence growing. "You know," she said, "Now that she's no longer with that attorney, it *would* be great to see her get out there again. To be with someone who understands her lifestyle." She finally looked over at Joe, who was watching her intently.

"Drink up," she said, pointing to his glass. "Or, if you want, I can make you some of that tea you love so much."

"No thanks on either count," he said, rising to take his glass back to the kitchen. "The tea will keep me up too long, the wine will knock me out too soon." Then he thought, *You'd do well to slow your roll on the wine yourself, lady.*

Walking past her toward the main staircase, he said, "I'm gonna hit the shower, then try heading to bed."

What Sissy could hear in the tone of Joe's voice was difficult to ascertain. What she did know was that her words were planting the appropriate seed of doubt in his mind. "Joe, are you okay," she asked.

Resting his hand on the banister, Joe hesitated. "Yeah, I'm good."

"You just tired or is there something you need to talk about?"

He did need to talk, but he wasn't in the mood to discuss it with her. Joe could tell Sissy was baiting him; perhaps hoping that he'd spill some info on his relationship with Maggie. He never could understand the underlying tension that seemed to exist between the two women. Perhaps Sissy was feeling protective of her baby sister's memory. Maybe it was an issue of territory.

Maybe his mother was right about Sissy all along, and he was simply oblivious to it.

It didn't matter. Joe was exhausted, and he wanted to talk to Maggie. He loved that she was in her element, working hard and happy doing it. But it made for a hard couple of months. As much as his head told him that he had nothing to fear between Maggie and Mr. Hotshot-Record-Producer Guy, Sissy's disclosure had left his heart feeling more than a little insecure.

Clearing his throat, he changed the subject. "Feel free to make yourself at home. You gonna camp out on the top floor?"

"Sure. Do you still have that old shirt?"

"Yeah. I'll leave it on that table in the hall."

"Thanks, Joe."

"Glad to have you. Sleep well."

"G'night."

Sissy leaned back into the soft cushions of the sofa and closed her eyes. She imagined the changes she would bring to the house. Or better yet, she thought of some of the homes of her colleagues: those massive structures in the upscale neighborhood of Brentwood. She could talk Joe into selling this old house for something newer, more modern. Somewhere that didn't have one trace of his previous life.

"Oh, what am I doing?" she said, shaking her head. She was getting way ahead of herself, and she knew it. Those things would come, in time. Even though she could still sense some sort of feeling for Maggie on Joe's part; in the nearly two months that she'd been in the studio, Sissy was making sure that *she* was the one that held Joe's attention.

As one of the two executive producers, Sissy's MO was simple: stretch out the creative process of Maggie's project for as long as possible without arousing suspicion or wasting too much money. She began by bringing in a succession of players and singers whom she knew wouldn't meet Fabian's standards. It took an extra week and a half to find the people that were perfect for the job. When questioned, she'd simply smile, convincing her superiors that she ultimately had Maggie's best interests at heart.

Sissy settled back and allowed the voluminous couch cushions to envelop her as she finished her wine. In the distance, she could hear the shower water running. Dispatching the last of her drink, she rose and helped herself to the glass that Joe had left on the countertop.

She was surprised at how little guilt she felt over her machinations. Perhaps it was all those years in the music industry game; doing what she had to do to get where and what she needed, with little concern for where it left others in her wake.

Tonight, as it had been for many nights, that thing she felt she needed was Joe Buchanan.

Of course there was no joy in the fact that she had to lose her sister to have this opportunity. But the fact of the matter was that Grace was indeed dead; and for Sissy, looking back was never a good use of her energy. As cold as it might seem, it was time for all of them to move on.

She was pleased with how she'd let Joe fester with the possibility that Maggie could actually take up with someone like Fabian - a man with whom she clearly had more in common. And now that the seed had been planted, it was only a matter of time before she would make her move.

Slowly, Sissy ascended the stairs, stopping at the door to the master bedroom. On a table next to the door, there was the old cotton shirt with the frayed collar she loved to wear when she stayed the night.

Lifting it to her nose, Sissy buried her face in the fabric and inhaled deeply. Her senses were slowly succumbing to the intense vibration that the wine was creating. Turning her head to the side, she leaned against the door, closed her eyes and smiled at the sound of Joe's slightly off-key hum of a pop song as the water continued to run. With a clear picture of Joe in her mind, she thought, *Tonight's the night. It's time.*

Chapter 12

Joe stepped through the door; a gust of wind hitting his face, momentarily taking his breath away. Looking out into the vast waving field before him, he saw her. He smiled as he descended the steps, his pace increasing with every stride.

Adorned in white, Maggie's soft curls floated in the breeze as she turned to face him. Her skin glowed with the color of burnished gold, her smile, impossibly radiant. The breeze lifted the gauzy material of her dress around her, as if she were seated in the center of a cloud. She extended her hand to him, and he eagerly accepted. With his other hand, Joe encircled Maggie's waist. He slowly began his contact with soft kisses on her cheeks, her nose, her forehead.

As the wind whipped around them, they began their embrace. Their kiss deepening, they took no notice of the darkening skies above them. The intensity of their passion equaled the frenzy of the growing storm.

A crash of thunder, a flash of lightning, the wind quickly gained strength, the sky now ominous shades of green and grey. Suddenly, the power of the storm ripped them apart, spinning Joe around and disorienting him. Gaining his bearings, he realized that Maggie was nowhere to be found.

His calls to her futilely lost in the fury of the storm, Joe began to panic. He searched for the door from which he came, but there was nothing but open space, violent winds and angry ribbons of lightning splitting the sky.

A hand touched his shoulder from behind. As hope returned to his heart, and with Maggie's name on his lips, he was stunned into silence to see standing before him a woman of smaller carriage; sable-brown hair and the same gauzy white dress flying freely in the fearsome storm. His face now ashen, Joe can barely speak her name.

"Grace?"

She was barely visible beyond the flashing of the lightning, but he was most certainly looking into the face of his wife. Grace reached up and snaked one hand around to the back of his head, drawing him down to her. Familiarity replaced fear as his kiss deepened, separating only to breathlessly repeat her name.

"Grace...Grace...oh Grace…"

"Joe...I love you so much Joe," he could hear her say. *"I'll always be here for you. I'll never leave you. I love you, Joe..."*

It took several minutes for him to open his eyes and allow reality to take shape. The feminine tones of her voice became deeper, throatier, and somewhat slurred. "Oh Joe, tell me you love me, Joe…"

The strawberry blonde silk of Sissy's hair swept over his face, jarring him back to consciousness. With all the energy his body could muster, Joe twisted from beneath her, causing him to tumble from the bed.

"Sissy!" he whisper-shouted. "What is wrong with you, woman? What are you doing?"

Gathering the comforter around her, his sudden move left Sissy startled and dumbfounded. "I…I…I don't…" she stammered as she quickly began to sober.

She could see herself standing outside his bedroom door earlier that night, simply waiting for him to crawl into bed and fall asleep before she would join him. That was her plan...but somewhere in the waiting, the wine took over, and she fell asleep by the door. When she awoke, she was still slightly woozy from the wine, and had no idea how much time had passed. When she opened the door to Joe's bedroom, the steady rhythm of his breathing convinced her that he was asleep.

Doffing her shirt, she carelessly tossed it to the end of the bed and slipped beneath the sheets. The combination of the cool of the sheets and the musky warmth of Joe's body on her skin was exhilarating.

Shaking her head at the memory of her behavior, all she could manage to do was utter a weak, "Joe, I'm...I'm so..."

In any other scenario, Sissy would have made a fetching sight. Her perfectly conditioned hair had just enough seductive chaos to it; her lips pouting and full, her freckled skin a glowing ivory.

But it was in that terrifying moment that Joe realized their state of undress: him in boxer-briefs and Sissy wearing even less. Scrambling for his robe, he simultaneously tossed her the shirt that lay crumpled at the foot of the bed.

"Please put this on," he said, exasperated.

Mortified for totally different reasons, they turned their backs to one another as they quickly dressed. "I'm gonna ask you again," Joe said as he scrubbed his fingers through his hair and stared out the window. "What did you think we were going to do?"

Embarrassed and dejected, Sissy softly began to cry. "I'm sorry, Joe. I'm just so sorry."

The sound of her sobs triggered a sense of pity within him. He slowly walked to his side of the bed and sat down. The distance he kept was close enough to communicate care without sending any misleading signals. Her back still to him, she tried in vain to explain herself.

"When you kissed me back, I thought you knew it was me."

"Sissy, I was asleep," Joe said, "and if you don't mind my saying, you downed quite a bit of wine tonight."

Rising quickly, a humiliated Sissy ran for the door. "Sis," Joe pleaded. "C'mon. Talk to me. We *are* family, right? You're like my sister."

Stopping at the door, her hand on the knob, she paused momentarily. Hearing him say she was *like* a sister brought with it a nauseating familiarity. His use of the exact word that kept her nemesis on the outside looking in gave her the strength she needed to reconsider her escape. But the old bedroom door was stuck, and in her weakened state, proved difficult to open "I can't, Joe. I'm sorry. I'm gonna leave. I *have* to leave"

"No way you're leaving this house in the shape you're in," Joe said, walking toward her. "Go upstairs, sleep this off and we'll talk tomorrow. Okay?"

Sissy's nod was barely perceptible as she finally pulled the door open quickly and shut it behind her.

As her heard her footsteps softly ascending the stairs, his cell began to ring. Looking at the clock on his nightstand, he saw the time was 11:05. Joe knew that it was Maggie on the phone. His nerves still frayed, he debated whether or not he should answer.

Joe knew he was merely a victim of circumstance; yet his body's response to Sissy left him feeling a tremendous amount of guilt and anguish. He decided to take the call, but after a heavy intake of air, Joe answered his phone with perhaps a bit too much gusto.

"Hey there Mags!" he exclaimed. "What's going on with you? Me? Nothing, just hanging out, not doing anything at all. What do you mean I sound weird? No, no, you didn't wake me."

At least that was the truth.

The house was silent as Sissy crept down the stairs. She decided to stay out of the way until Joe and the children had left for the morning before heading for home herself.

The scent of coffee beckoned her to the kitchen where a mug, a glass of water, two aspirin and two vitamin B tablets on a napkin were sitting on the countertop. A nearby note read: *"to cure what is probably ailing you. Joe."* She grimaced at his attempt at humor.

She took the vitamins, finished the water and sat at the kitchen table with the mug of coffee, churning with anger and humiliation. At herself for being so reckless. At Joe for not realizing a good thing when he had it right in front of him. At Maggie for her constant presence in Sissy's life.

"Ugh!" Sissy exclaimed as her head went into her hands. Her thoughts were interrupted when she heard the garage door open. Before she was able to escape the kitchen for the bonus room, Joe came through the back door.

"Hey, hey, whoa," he said as she started to get up.

"Joe, I am so sorry. I'll be out of here in just a minute..."

"Sissy, wait, *please*! Seriously, let's talk about last night. I want to understand."

Sissy stopped in the doorway and turned reluctantly

to face him. He motioned toward the kitchen table where they both took a seat.

Joe sprang back up to fix himself some coffee as a realization hit Sissy. "I thought you had back to back classes this morning," she said, her head still down.

Joe turned to look at her and chuckled out loud. "Um, I did. I came back to grab an early lunch. It's 11 am, Sis."

Sissy looked at the clock, returned her head to her hands and groaned. Joe laughed a little louder.

"Shhh…" she pleaded. "That's too loud."

"I take it the aspirin hasn't kicked in yet?"

"No," she moaned. "I just took it. We can talk. Just softly, okay?"

"So tell me, what in the world is going on with you?"

"I don't know, Joe," she began. "I think I'm just lonely. I've spent so many years married to my work, to this industry. When I moved back here from California, I wanted a fresh start. And you've always been so kind to me…"

"Well of course," Joe interjected. "You're Grace's sister, and the children's aunt. Why wouldn't I be good to you?"

"I know, I know. I think I just lost my head in all that wine. I'm sorry. I hope that you don't hold this against me," she said earnestly.

"Not in the least," he said, smiling. "I'm sorry if my actions misled you. I really do care about you, but right now, that's the best I can give."

A sharp pang of disappointment worked its way through Sissy's chest as the truth was finally laid out onto the table. Yet within the finality of his words, she still somehow managed to feel a small spark of hope…*right now, that's the best I can give.*

Stubbornly, she determined within herself that this

small statement kept her foot squarely in the door. This was now officially a waiting game; but Joe was worth it. She would just have to find another approach.

"Okay," she said. She rose from her place and poured the remainder of her coffee in the sink. "Well, since I've slept away most of the morning, I should probably see what I can do about the rest of my day. I'm sure my office is coming completely unhinged." The two of them laughed. Fumbling at the belt of the bathrobe, Sissy extended her hand to shake Joe's.

Joe took her hand and gave her a loving look. "We're cool, right," he asked.

"Of course we are."

Their hands still joined, she leaned in to kiss him chastely on the cheek. With his back to the door, only Sissy was able to see the figure standing outside preparing to come in. As her lips met the side of Joe's face, her eyes connected with those of a dumbfounded Maggie; whose arm was still raised to knock on the door.

Maggie had been surfing around on Facebook over breakfast when she came upon a post she'd read that morning on Joe's page about heading home for an early lunch. "Not sure which is more dangerous," it read. "Cafeteria food or what comes out of my own kitchen. Better stick with the devil you know."

She decided to surprise him with some sandwiches she'd picked up, hoping to steal some time with him before heading into the studio to work. The surprise, as it would seem, was definitely on Maggie.

Frozen, she watched helplessly as Sissy, clothed in a robe that was obviously Joes, slipped her arm around Joe's neck in a warm embrace. As the two women locked eyes, Maggie could see a definite look of triumph glowing from

Sissy's face. In the distance, a neighbor's dog barked, snapping Maggie from her trance. She backed away from the door slowly, and ran down the footpath back to her car.

Hands shaking, Maggie struggled not to cry. Finally getting the key in the ignition, she tore out onto the highway with the speed of a NASCAR champion.

"That explains why you sounded so strange last night," she muttered to the air. "I guess I would sound strange too if someone were in my bed…"

In his profession, Blake Fabian had pretty much seen it all, both on stage and off. From marital spats to lovers' quarrels; inebriated musicians and coked-out groupies, there was little to nothing in the world of entertainment that fazed him.

Nashville was always a breath of fresh air to him. Although the seedy underbelly of the music scene existed just as readily as it did anywhere else, in Tennessee it was less inclined to rear its head right away. The prevailing ethic seemed to be: work first, party later. Nashville's charm always reminded him of why he got into this business in the first place. He could do his job without the stereotypical distractions of the fast lane…while still finding those avenues to pick up a little action 'off the clock' should he ever feel the need to cut loose.

He considered that January invitation from Lanie to helm a Music City project a total lark. While he valued Lanie's opinion, he questioned her judgment when she directed him toward the website of a studio singer named Maggie West. Before even heading to her site, his first thoughts were of an aging wannabe.

But all preconceived notions diminished when he clicked on the icon that housed samples of her work. This woman was no wannabe. A little long in the tooth by industry standards to be sure; but the face, the voice…there was no escaping that "it factor."

"Looks like that *sheila*'s really got me over a barrel this time," he laughed as he continued to envelope himself in the smoothness of Maggie's sound. All the while, he couldn't stop staring at a simple yet dramatic black and white of Maggie sitting backward on a chair. "There is no escaping this."

From that moment on, Blake Fabian became a man obsessed. He could not get to Nashville quickly enough.

And just as he'd hoped, the ride was better than he'd ever dreamed. Maggie and Blake were a match made in musical heaven. He produced her, coached her, offered suggestions for her songs that she had never considered, all the while entertaining insights of her own that proved to be sheer genius. They both knew that each and every song had moved beyond the potential to be radio friendly hits, into the realm of complete works of art.

Maggie herself felt as though she were floating above a surreal situation. She couldn't believe how well the two of them clicked both professionally and personally. She laughed openly at Blake's persistent flirtations, never taking them seriously, yet basking in every word. The playful give and take of her witty refusals to what Blake considered some of his smoothest moves kept the atmosphere light and fun, while still getting the necessary work completed.

The time flew by, and while Maggie hated to see it end, the thing that fueled her fire was the thought of having regular time with Joe again. Though the process was exhilarating, she'd missed him and the children terribly.

But on what should have been a celebratory final afternoon of recording, there was a perceptible shift in Maggie's demeanor. It wasn't lost on anyone in the room - least of all, Blake Fabian.

"Hey Gregg, cut her mic for me, would ya, buddy?" Blake asked as he headed into the booth where she sat quietly.

With long, purposeful strides, he entered the dimly-lit area and sat on a stool in front of her, resting his hands on his knees. The green of his eyes deepened as his gaze narrowed with genuine concern.

"Well, there was a little bit of magic here and there, but I'm really not liking the idea of piecing together stuff from all these different tracks. What's up with my little one-take wonder?"

Maggie found it difficult to spell out exactly what she was feeling at the time. As she opened her mouth to speak, she noticed Sissy had entered the studio. She was dressed in a smart khaki colored mini skirt with a matching jacket that Maggie was fairly certain she'd worn the day before. The only difference was the emerald green cotton shirt she wore underneath. Given what Maggie had witnessed just a few hours before, she would have bet her next paycheck that the shirt Sissy wore was borrowed...from Joe.

Chatting breezily with the men in the control area, Sissy removed the jacket with the express intention of seeing if Maggie would recognize it. And she did.

The shirt was a gift; purchased by his mother, selected by Maggie. This was no accident or coincidence. Sissy knew exactly what she was doing. In one solitary action, she'd managed to slap both Maggie and Elise at the same time. And while she could only see Maggie in silhouette,

Sissy was certain Maggie felt the blow.

She did.

"Sometimes girls just get a little blue," she said, knowing that her explanation was as lame as it sounded coming out of her. "I can do this. Let's get back to work."

"You know what?" Blake said. "We are so far ahead of schedule, I think we can afford to slow things down a bit. How 'bout we knock off till tomorrow and I take you out for a great meal tonight. You pick, I pay."

The tears that had bubbled at Maggie's eyes began to spill over. "I don't know if I'd be very good company, B," she said, slowly rising to her feet. Wiping her eyes, she continued. "Seriously, let's go. I can do this."

Standing directly in front of her, he placed his hands on her shoulders. "You sure?"

"Yeah, I'm sure." Maggie's smile brightened tentatively.

"Okay then," Blake said. "Let's take five. You stay right there and get yourself together. Uncle Blake's gonna take care of things."

Maggie wiped more tears from her eyes while laughing, "Please don't call yourself 'Uncle Blake.' That's so creepy."

Blake knew his charm was having an effect. Despite his reputation as a womanizer, he'd grown sincerely fond of Maggie. He respected her abilities, but mostly, he respected her as a person. He earnestly cared about her. With a hearty chuckle, he walked back out of the room as confidently as he entered it.

Maggie sipped the now-lukewarm tea from a paper cup as she watched Blake usher everyone from the control room except Gregg, the engineer. She couldn't help but smile when she saw Sissy attempt to resist the order to vacate. Watching Sissy move from flirtation, to authority, to outright anger was more than amusing to Maggie. It was downright satisfying. But despite her efforts Blake managed to gently take her by the arm and lead her out of the room.

For a long time Blake didn't return. Maggie could see his shadow pacing back and forth behind the door in the front lobby; she could only surmise that he was "taking care of things" as he'd suggested.

Another fleeting memory of Grace - instructing her to do just that. Maggie could hear her best friend's voice: *I need you...to take care of things...* A sad smile momentarily shadowed Maggie's face.

Figuring the coast was clear of curious onlookers, she emerged from the booth to freshen her cup of tea. As she and Gregg engaged in conversation, she could hear bits of Blake's rather animated exchange over the phone. Finally, the door leading to the lobby opened, and he came back.

"All right, good on ya, mate," he said cheerfully as he flashed a winning smile in Maggie's direction. Ignoring her questioning expression, he held up a finger to indicate that he was nearly done with his conversation.

"Fantastic. Right. See you then. Bye." Turning his attention to Maggie, he said "Okay, love, ready to try again?"

"On one condition."

Blake's brow furrowed, "Okay..." he said, drawing out the word slowly.

"Tell me what it you were doing out there? What 'things' are you taking care of?"

"Aww, now that's for me to know and you to find out."

He pointed in the direction of the recording booth. "After you get back to work."

Maggie was already beginning to feel better. With a slow, skeptical turn, she returned to the recording booth. "Okay, okay. You're the boss," she said.

"And don't you forget it."

The music began again, and with her spirits buoyed, Maggie found what she needed to give the song what it needed. With each note, she could feel the life coursing through her wounded spirit. She never missed a beat, a note or a change of key.

Gregg sat in astonishment as the notes poured out of her into the microphone, and out through the speakers, directly into a part of him that few vocalists had been able to penetrate. He'd seen and heard it all too. Very little impressed him. Until Maggie West.

Muttering an obscenity, he shook his head and looked up at Blake, who stood braced against the edge of the control board. "I'm tellin' you, Fabian," he said in a cigarette-laden drawl. "We're gonna have to come up with a whole new word for good. That's how amazing this chick is."

With the edges of his lips curled in a proprietary smile, Blake's face took on a mystical glow. Without returning the look, he responded to Gregg's assertion. "You got that right, buddy. You certainly got that right."

"Blake Fabian, what on earth is all of this?"

Maggie stood at the door to the studio green room in awe. A space that was normally reserved for musicians to chat during all too brief breaks while drinking overdone coffee, had been transformed into an intimate dream.

Blake had worked his magic by arranging a richly hued display of throw pillows, wall draping and candles of every size and shape on candlesticks, plates and pedestals.

To compliment this feast for the eyes were the equally warm and delicious scents of turmeric, garlic and cinnamon. As he removed silver lids from their platters, Maggie shook her head in stunned silence; her face frozen in surprise and wonder.

"Moroccan?"

"Yep."

Throwing up her hands, she said, "Amazing what you can do with a few simple phone calls."

Blake curled his fingers toward his face, breathed on his nails and with exaggerated nonchalance, buffed them on his shoulder.

"How did you get this together in such a short time?" she asked.

His voice took on that of a German accent as he rubbed his hands together, "Oh I have my *veys.*"

Suddenly, another recollection flashed across Maggie's consciousness: Joe standing before her in the airport, sweetly clutching a handful of her favorite flowers saying the exact same thing when she asked him how he managed to find them at Christmas time.

That memory was far more painful and her smile slowly faded.

Aw, no…no, no, no!!" Blake exclaimed, fully prepared to turn on an undiluted display of pure Aussie charm. "No sad *sheilas* tonight. Nope, tonight is all about good food…" He took her hands in his and led her toward an assembly of plush pillows and eased her into a comfortable seating position. No sooner did he get Maggie settle, than he was up once again, grasping a bottle of Pinot Noir.

With a soft *pop* of the cork, he continued with the evening's agenda. "…and good wine. I'll just let this breathe for a moment…" He produced two wine glasses along with the breathing beverage as he slowly lowered himself to sit directly across from her, a series of silk scarves serving as the tablecloth over what was normally a weathered thrift store coffee table.

He poured the wine with one hand, while negotiating a remote control with the other. Maggie's smile returned. She couldn't help but be impressed. The soft, poetic strains of what she was certain was George Morgan filled the air.

"…good, classic Country tunes… and most important… good conversation. Tonight, we celebrate the completion of Phase One of what I believe is going to be one of the most magical moments in the world of music."

Maggie's expression was one of appreciation, and she applauded his earnest presentation. Blake placed one arm in front, and one arm behind his back and bent at the waist. "Thank you, thank you. You're too kind." As he dished food onto her plate, he decided to shoot directly from the hip and get straight to the heart of what was troubling her. "Start from the top," he said. "And don't waste my time with any of that 'oh, I don't wanna bore you with my drama' crap. Not after I went through all of this for you."

She could hear the familiar joking in his tone. But she knew it masked the overall concern he had. So that's what she did: Starting with her earliest memories of Grace, she gave him every detail-the good, the bad, and the too painful to bear. He listened intently, nodded appropriately, and said very little; stopping only to ask questions for clarification.

In a rare moment of transparency, Maggie poured out

her soul. She cried on occasion, particularly when she approached the end of her story where she saw Sissy enter the control booth that morning wearing what Maggie was certain was the shirt that belonged to Joe.

At the story's end, Blake sat still and thoughtfully contemplated all that he'd just heard. Taking a sip of his wine, he paused before responding. With a look of total seriousness on his face, he finally said, "So, what you're saying is that I never had a bleedin' chance with you?"

His attempt at levity to lighten her spirits was a huge gamble; and luckily for him, it paid off. Maggie leaned forward, her arms resting on the table. "You do realize you've got *serious* issues, right?" she asked, once again coming toe to toe with his deadpan delivery.

"The word 'unbalanced' has been used on more than one occasion, yes."

"Okay. As long as were clear on that point."

The two of them broke into laughter as she threw a small piece of bread in his direction. Dodging it, he replied, "Hey, you don't want to get into a food fight with me. Not only would you lose, but I'm starving, and this stuff's too good to go to waste!"

As their laughter subsided, he reached across the table and took her hand in his. "Okay, time for truth. I know you're going to think I'm just delivering a line to get on your good side, but I've gotta tell ya, Maggie, you're the real deal. Not just as a singer, or even as a songwriter - you are one of the best people I know. These past few weeks have been some of the most fun I've ever had. So I know that even though I've shamelessly hit on you all this time…"

"Shameless is a perfect word, Blake," she cut in.

"Hush now, this is a rare moment of concession for

me. I hate to lapse into the clichéd 'you deserve someone as great, if not greater than you,' blah, blah, blah. But, *crikey*, lady, someone should have snatched you up a long time ago. And I'm only willing to back off because I know you're heart is set on this Joe bloke, who, by the way, I don't think even remotely deserves you."

"He's not a bad guy, Blake," Maggie interrupted once again. "In fact, I think if you met him, you'd like him too."

"Fat chance!" Blake exclaimed. "No way am I gonna be friends with a rival."

Maggie rolled her eyes, "You are not a well person."

"Maggie…" Blake said as he smiled and brought her hand to his lips. Maggie basked in the attention as he kissed her hand.

Joe tried to process what he was witnessing between Blake and Maggie. He could see directly into the green room from the front door of the studio. He knew this was the final day of recording for her, so when her phone went directly to voice mail, he wasn't surprised. What did surprise him, however, was that she'd not returned any of his calls. He thought that an impromptu celebratory dinner would be a great way for them to reconnect. But he could also see the décor, the candles, the food…and he could see the smile on Maggie's face as Blake Fabian tenderly kissed her hand; never letting it go, even when he brought it to rest on the table.

The conversation was obviously one of an intimate nature - that much was hard to hide. And Sissy's words came back to Joe:

…the man is a charmer. I can't think of one woman on the planet who hasn't been blindsided by that accent…

…now that she's no longer with that attorney, it would be great to see her get out there again, ya know? To be with someone

who understands her lifestyle...

"So," Joe said softly as he shoved his hands in his pockets. "I guess that's that then."

For a moment, he hesitated. For a moment, he considered pounding on the door and demanding an explanation.

Instead, he chose to believe what Sissy had said. A familiar ache returned to the center of Joe's chest, the lump in his throat refusing to abate. He didn't know much about Maggie's world; but one of the things he loved about her was her detachment from it. She seemed unspoiled by it. He had already decided that fame and fortune were in her future, but she would be one of the few who would still be a 'regular girl,' with time and room in her circle for all of those she'd considered important.

Never in all the time he'd known Maggie did he even remotely consider that he would be out of that circle...until now.

Declan was dumbfounded. "Wow," was all he could manage to say. Slowly shaking his head, he continued to munch on the remainder of his salad. The two of them were finishing their lunch in Joe's office, when the whole story was laid out in detail.

"I guess Sissy had the whole thing down cold," Joe said testily. "This Fabian guy walks her walk, talks her language. Maybe they are a better fit, I don't know…"

"Um, Jose - that 'wow' wasn't for Maggie and Crocodile Dundee," Declan said. "That 'wow' was for you."

The comment caught Joe off guard.

"What?"

"What do you mean, what? You just stood there

outside the door and did nothing?"

"I didn't know what to do."

Declan shook his head again and set the plastic container that held the remnants of his salad on the desk. He stared at his friend. "Yeah, like I said - wow. In all the years I've known you, I don't think I've ever seen you cave this quickly. Who *are* you?"

With a pained expression, Joe got up from his desk and walked toward the window. Mindlessly twirling a piece of string between his index fingers, he said: "Yeah, I totally wimped out on this. I just didn't think I could compete with that guy."

"Listen bud," Declan said, "I *am* that guy. I know what people see on the outside is pretty much how I'm judged, and I don't fight it. I know it affords me certain liberties with the females of the world..."

"Are you trying to get me to hate you now?"

"I'm serious. You were the one who was holding out for the right girl; you weren't into dating around. In your relationships, what few there were, you gave it everything you had, because you were hoping it would lead to somewhere with a white picket fence. But the marriage and baby thing wasn't my scene, so, like that guy, I played the field. And it didn't get old. Still isn't. I like the way my cards are stacked."

"Declan, get to the part that supposed to make me feel better. *Now.*"

"Okay, here it is: When I started seeing you and Maggie together, there was no, 'this is weird,' thing. It should have been; Maggie was, well, you know...Maggie. Like our sister. Cool hang, fun gal, easy on the eyes, but she was Maggie - the other half of the "Maggie and Grace Show."

Joe nodded in understanding.

"But you guys have a chemistry that doesn't happen every day," Declan continued. "You know how to be best friends, because you've been working at it forever. But even though you've not announced anything to the world, I could see the love coming from a mile away. I'm surprised nobody's called you two on it."

Joe chuckled as he recalled the conversation he had with his mother over the Christmas holiday. "Is it that obvious?"

"Starving dogs in front of raw meat are more subtle."

Joe turned from the window and regarded what Declan was saying as the latter continued. "You guys have history. You've been through hell and back together; those roots go deep. But if you honestly think that you weathered all the stops and starts of the last few months only to have her bail out now, just because some guy comes along..." Declan's face took on a far away expression. "Granted, I've seen him. He kinda reminds me of me..."

"Deck!" Joe said with a slight irritation.

"Sorry. I was kinda messin' with you there. Anyway, Maggie's true blue in my opinion. You just let the big blonde guy win by default."

Joe leaned with his back to the window sill, running his hands through his hair the way he always did when he was trying to regain his focus. He emitted a throaty groan in exasperation.

"I think I'm in love with her, Deck," Joe said quietly. "There was no drama with her, just easy peace. I can handle the music and the road life taking her away for periods at a time. I just can't handle her not being around at all."

"Then what are you waiting for," Declan asked "Go to her. She deserves a face-to-face talk."

Sissy had a plan. But things weren't going according to plan. The wedge that Maggie's career had placed between her and Joe was fortuitous, and Sissy was doing her best to capitalize on that. What Maggie thought she saw that morning in Joe's kitchen and what Joe thought he saw between Maggie and Blake Fabian were a set of fantastic coincidences that only seemed to help said plan along. And with Sissy leading the charge at Star Records to get the promotional end of things for Maggie underway, there was no time for them to get to the heart of anything. The grueling, grass-roots endeavor that was Maggie's radio tour took her out of town and on the road almost immediately.

This was all part of Sissy's plan, and under normal circumstances, it would have won her a spot in that empty space the Buchanans possessed.

But it didn't. In fact, the exact opposite was happening. And it was maddening. Her mind went back to a day in the past week when she was sitting with the children around their dinner table. She had worked hard to cook them something she thought they'd like. But there aren't too many children that are drawn to Sissy's sophisticated tastes.

Young Gwen tried to be diplomatic. "Aunt Sissy, it's not that we don't like your cooking…"

"We just don't *understand* your cooking," said Matty.

"Matty," Gwen hissed, "Shut up! That's not nice!"

"Sorry. When she said we were having 'coco-van,' I was thinking we were finally getting something chocolate for dinner."

"I miss Aunt Maggie's baked chicken," said M&M quietly. "When she made dinner, it felt like Thanksgiving all the time."

"I miss Aunt Maggie," said Matty.

Gwen could see the dejection on her aunt's face, and quickly tried to lighten the mood. "Now guys, Aunt Sissy worked real hard on this, and it *is* chicken, little sister, so let's try it, okay? Aunt Sissy, I think it smells really good. Come on nerds, dig in!"

The children ate their meal; at first tentatively, but finally cleaned their plates. Sissy was grateful, but irritated that she was being compared to Maggie yet again - and failing miserably.

As the dinner progressed, each child was full of questions and comments about Maggie and her time away.

"When is she coming home?"

"Is she getting famous?"

"What's the fun in eating my vegetables if she's not fussing at me?"

"When she called last week for our birthday, we talked to her for like, *ever!*"

"I know! She even helped me with an English assignment over the phone."

It was during this dinnertime conversation that a profound truth became crystal clear to Sissy: to the children, Maggie was love; she was merely a baby sitter.

And then there was Joe.

In the months since Maggie's departure, there was the lingering awareness on Sissy's part that she was becoming more like the guest who had overstayed her welcome, than the savior she had hoped to be.

Having her around did make things easier; but Joe was finally able to see that his sister-in-law was holding out hope for something more from him, despite their talk a few weeks back.

The demands of his life, his inability to reach Maggie, and Sissy's questionable motives collided in a perfect storm one morning as he descended the stairs to find her in the kitchen cleaning up after breakfast.

"Don't you ever go home," he asked wearily, barely cognizant of what he'd said.

Sissy felt as though she'd been slapped with a wet towel. "Um...I'm sorry, Joe..." She quickly attempted to leave the kitchen, her work unfinished.

Joe realized his harshness and immediately backpedaled. "Wait, Sissy. I'm sorry. Come back, please."

Sissy stopped just past him at the doorway. Without looking at him she said, "No, Joe, you're right. I didn't mean to overstep. You call me when you need me, okay?"

"Miss Hammond. Miss Hammond?"

Sissy had been reading the same paragraph for the better part of twenty minutes. The perky young blonde intern was standing in front of her desk; a cup of coffee in one hand, and a stack of trade magazines in the other. She attempted to break through Sissy's wall once again. Her words were louder and more deliberate, with a slight tremolo of nervousness at having to elevate her tone:

"Miss Hammond!"

Sissy startled at the sound, "Wha?! Oh, my word, Becky, you scared me! What do you want?"

"I...I'm sorry, Miss Hammond, you were just so deep in thought. I brought the trades you asked for that had articles about Maggie West's radio tour.

Sissy regrouped and took a sip of tea. "Oh darling, I'm sorry. I didn't mean to yell. Yes, I was deep in thought.

Hand me those magazines dear. And again, I apologize."

Becky's fear dissolved in the light of Sissy's changed mood. "Oh no problem, Ms. H. I took the liberty to stick post-it strips on the pages that talk about her so you can find them easier. Looks like she's really kickin' butt out there. Everybody loves her!"

Sissy managed a smile that would be considered less than sincere by anyone who knew her well. Frozen in place, her lips barely moved when she spoke.

"Yes," she said as she drew out the word. "Thank you dear. I think that's all I have for you today."

"Oh, one more thing, Ms. H. Ms. Hoyos wanted me to give you a heads up on the meeting with Maggie's management concerning her showcase at The Factory."

Sissy felt that if she heard Maggie West's name again, her head would implode. "Uh-huh," she said as she flipped through the trades. "Got the e-mail, but thanks for the reminder."

"The time's been changed," Becky said. Looking at her cell phone clock she said, "You've got about 25 minutes."

"Fine," Sissy said. She looked up briefly. "Anything else?" she said, trying to sound pleasant.

"No ma'am."

Closing the magazine and pulling a file from her drawer, she said, "Okay then. Now I'm done with you."

The same frozen smile was on her face, but for Becky, its meaning felt darker and much more ominous. Nervously, she scurried away.

Down the hall, Becky could be heard breathlessly greeting Blake Fabian in the way that most young women greeted Blake Fabian.

"Yes, she's in her office," Becky said with the ardor of a teen in the presence of her favorite idol. As Blake appeared in the hallway, stifled giggles could be heard fading into the distance.

"Gwen, you flaxen-haired beauty," Blake cooed, still basking in the glow of the attention he was receiving at the other end of the hallway. "So good to see you again."

Sissy was in no mood. "What do you want, Fabian? I've got a meeting in less than half an hour and I need to get my ducks in a row."

"Yes, I know. I'm in on it too. It's about Maggie's showcase. I'm going to be serving as a production consultant for the video."

"Video?"

"Yeah, that's what the meeting's about. I was able to convince the folks at CMT to tape an hour long broadcast. Got some great sponsors lined up, and a few top acts to come sit in with her…"

Sissy sat back and crossed one leg over another. "Well aren't you just the hero of the day," she said sarcastically. "You and Maggie are just poised to be the next power couple, aren't you?"

"Seriously, lady, what's your problem with Maggie?"

"I have no problem with…her." she said, unable to even speak her name.

"Well you've got me scratchin' my head on this one, because with any other artist, you'd be looking for your spot on the carcass to sink your teeth for your share of the glory. I don't think I've ever seen you so hesitant or unwilling to be part of things."

"Well, I'm sure Country Music's newest sweetheart can fill you in the next time you have a nice romantic night out…or, rather *in*."

"What?"

Sissy stood up and began to collect the materials she'd

need for her meeting. "Oh, come on. Everyone knows it was business as usual with the ol' Aussie," she cracked. "You sweep in to Nashville; pour on your "G'day" charm, and bam! Maggie's wrapped around your little finger."

Blake felt the feminine claws come out in Sissy's words, and was in no mood for a catfight. But she was making this so easy that he couldn't resist. He figured with 15 minutes to kill, he might as well have a witch for breakfast.

He closed the door.

"Sure, I pulled some strings a few weeks back and laid out a nice spread for her at the studio."

Sissy scoffed, "Wow, that's a great way of putting it."

The sophomoric nature of her statement caused Blake to grimace in disgust. He went on. "That was to cheer her up after a hard day's work. That was after she told me *her* story - about her best friend, and a guy named Joe - her family, your family, a story that ended with her seeing the two of you in his kitchen…"

Sissy slowed her pace, eventually stopped and looked Blake in the eye. Blake took that as permission to continue; he knew he'd hit the mark.

"So if you wanna talk about someone sweeping in and ruining someone's love life, Ms. Pot, watch what you say to the ol' kettle here."

Sissy stammered in her defense, but was unable to formulate a reasonable explanation.

"What was that deal with you showing up at the studio wearing that guy's shirt," Blake asked.

It seemed that Maggie held nothing back in her recollection to Blake. A nearly unrecognizable pang of guilt over her actions caused Sissy's frustration to reach fever pitch.

"What Joe and I share is none of your business," she half shouted.

"What you and Joe share sounds like it's all in your head," he said, leaning against the wall.

Muttering an obscenity, Sissy rushed past him. "Shut up, Blake. It's time for the meeting."

Chapter 13

E ntering her grandparent's library, Gwen sat next to Joe on the sofa in the middle of the room. "Hey there, kiddo," he said as cheerfully as he could.

Gwen had been studying her father closely in the weeks following Maggie's departure. His sadness was evident, despite his attempts at covering his feelings. But his eldest child could tell that he was feeling the void as deeply as she and her siblings were.

The trip to the Hammond's house was meant to be an opportunity for the kids to spend a much needed weekend with their grandparents. It also afforded Joe the chance at a temporary break from any and all reminders of what he felt he had lost with Maggie.

"Daddy, can I talk to you for a second?"

"Of course. What's on your mind?"

"Well…you, mostly."

"Me?"

Gwen nodded slowly as she curled her legs under herself on the couch. "Yeah. The twins and I were talking…"

"Oh boy," he said with a furrowed brow. "A meeting of the minds? That's scary."

"I'm serious, Daddy. We know you're sad 'cause you're missing Aunt Maggie."

Joe's expression conveyed acquiescence.

"You guys had a fight, didn't you?"

"More like a really intense disagreement."

"What about?"

"Grown up stuff," Joe said, taking her hand. "Nothing you need to get concerned about."

"It's been like, forever since she's come to see us."

"Well, her singing career is keeping her busy. You know, like when she was with Miss Timmons. But these days, she's doing her own songs, so now she's gotta work a little harder."

"Is that what you guys fought about?"

"Sort of."

Gwen's eyes narrowed and she drew away her hand. "That's a load of bull, Dad."

His daughter's comment immediately sparked Joe's anger. "Gwyneth Michelle Buchannan, that's no way to speak to any grownup, much less your father," he chided.

"I'm not trying be disrespectful," she said immediately. "But you're always telling us that the truth is more important than anything. And I don't think you're telling me the truth."

Her ability to get to the heart of a situation moved Joe deeply. She came by it honestly - something else inherited directly from her mother.

"Dad," She continued. "I think you and Aunt Maggie like each other, I mean, like, boyfriend-and-girlfriend like each other. And I think that's why you fought."

Joe shook his head in disbelief. "Did Maggie say as much to you?"

"Heck no," Gwen said. "I could just see the way you guys would look each other all the time. All the time we spent together. You were happy, jokey and fun to be around. Now, you just mope all over the house. It's depressing."

"You can tell all of that?"

"Hey, I'm a kid, but I'm not stupid," she said.

"No, sweet girl, you kids are anything and everything except stupid, that's for sure," he said as he leaned back and stared at the ceiling.

"And it's the same with Aunt Maggie. Now when she calls us, it's cool and all, but when she asks how you are, it's in a sad way."

Gwen looked at him with pure pleading in her eyes. "What happened, Daddy?"

"Well, I guess we'd better talk about it then, huh?"

"Can we? 'Cause one minute we're happy with Mom, then we were sad 'cause she died. Then Aunt Maggie kept us happy, then we were sad again 'cause she went away."

"Thanks for the recap."

"I do have another question though."

"Shoot."

"Why does Aunt Sissy hate Aunt Maggie?"

The question, while logical, shocked Joe because he had no idea just how much his children actually saw.

"Hate's a pretty strong word, kiddo."

"That's how we see it," Gwen said. She started playing with a rubber band that had been on her wrist. Before it became a distraction, Joe took it from her.

"What did exactly did you see?"

"Welllll…." Gwen was hesitant to tell the whole truth, but since she knew she'd begun the conversation, she owed it to her dad to tell him everything. "It was mostly me and M&M. We'd hear things…phone calls Aunt Sissy would make when she'd babysit us. I'd hear her call Aunt Maggie names; then talk about how she was trying to…um, what's the word...*hone* in on Aunt Sissy's territory."

Her usage of the word 'hone' had a questioning tone to it, as if she doing her best to quote correctly.

Joe's eyes widened in disbelief. Gwen's story was plausible; it sounded like a word Sissy would use.

Gwen continued. "There were some words used I don't really wanna say...but I could tell that Aunt Sissy was jealous...and...and..."

"And what?"

"I think Aunt Sissy wants to be your girlfriend too."

That was all Joe needed to hear. The fact that his mother, Maggie and his own child could see what he could not gave him a sick feeling of embarrassment.

"Gwen," Joe began slowly. "Aunt Sissy is your mom's sister. And she is pretty and funny and smart. But no matter what she may or may not want, that's all she is to me. *Like* a sister. Do you understand?"

Gwen nodded.

"Did you *want* her to be my girlfriend," he asked cautiously.

Gwen crinkled her nose in thought. "Um...I dunno. No, I guess. It doesn't feel right for some reason. I mean, I'm with you - she is so much fun when she babysits. But she's *Aunt* Sissy. I couldn't see her in a million years being my mom."

There was silence between the two of them that lasted for several seconds before she added, "But what about Maggie?"

Her deliberate omission of the title *Aunt* took Joe by surprise. He could tell that she was trying to have an adult conversation, so he responded in kind.

"Maggie...well...Maggie..."

"Yes Dad, Maggie." Gwen couldn't hide her smile as

she watched her father squirm at the thought of answering the question.

"Okay, okay. Maggie," he laughed. "I've always thought the world of her…she's amazing."

The innocuous nature of their exchange was beginning to wear on the teen. "Dad," she said sighing. "Answer my question! And don't lie, 'cause I can tell."

Again, Joe considered his words carefully. "How would *you* feel about us dating?"

"Honestly?"

"Seriously? You're pulling the 'honestly' thing on me after all this? Yes, Gwennie. Honestly."

"She's gotta be the single coolest person on the planet. And I miss her. And I think it would be totally cool for her to be your girlfriend…or…"

"Or…?"

"Don't make me say it, Dad. The thought of you having a love life is kinda gross 'cause you're so old. But yeah, I think she'd make a cool mom."

Once again, Joe shook his head and laughed out loud. Gathering her in his arms, he quickly put her in a headlock and proceeded to rub her head with his fist.

"Dad. A noogie? Seriously? Ugh! Quit it!"

Janice sipped her coffee as she leaned against the wall just outside the library. A sad smile formed on her lips as she considered the conversation that had just taken place between her son-in-law and grandchild.

"Matthew," she said to her husband as he walked by, newspaper in hand. "Can you come upstairs with me? I need to talk to you about something."

It was a brief conversation; Janice spilling the details of what she heard about Joe, Maggie and Sissy. Matthew was less concerned about the romance, and more about how Sissy's machinations and cruelty went unchecked.

"Don't worry about our daughter," Janice said with an uncharacteristic sternness. "I'll have a word with her."

"We need to talk to Dex and Lenore," Matthew said. "I'm curious to hear what they know."

The conversation with Maggie's parents was intense at the start; Dexter and Lenore seemed to know as little, if not less than what the Hammonds knew.

Dexter's countenance was on edge; he'd long harbored concerns that something like this could happen, and said as much.

"What do you mean, Dex?" Matthew asked.

"That girl has constantly been living up in her best friend's life from the moment they met. It's as though she couldn't get a life of her own."

"Okay, I'm going to skate by the fact that you are accusing our daughter of something you've been doing all along," Lenore exclaimed at her husband. "What I can't believe is that I hear you actually insinuating that Maggie had planned this! Please tell me you're not about to put any kind of blame on her!"

"Dex, Lenore...please," Janice said. "This isn't about blame. We just want the kids to be happy."

"Dex," Matthew said. "This isn't an easy situation for any of us. But we're going on two years since Gracie's passing. We know that Maggie wasn't waiting in the wings, or biding her time. She was just always there, and given the closeness of their friendship, it was just a matter of circumstance."

Janice reached across the table. She said, "Joe getting into another relationship was inevitable. That boy mates for life. The fact that it was Maggie just caught us off guard."

Matthew nodded in agreement. "Dexter," he said. "You are my brother. You have been since the day we became friends. And even though I wondered at first, race *isn't* the issue here."

Dexter was taken aback. Aside from the occasional joke between the two of them, he never once felt any sort of racial tension between him and his friend and fellow jurist. "*At first?*" he asked, his surprise evident.

"To be completely honest...yes, *at first,*" Matthew said quietly. "But we've known Maggie since she was a teenager. We adore her. There's no way this is about a Black and White thing."

"Of course not," Janice chimed in. "This goes so much deeper than race. We are in an extraordinary set of circumstances here."

"None of this was planned..." Matthew continued. "We didn't plan to lose Grace. We didn't plan for Joe and Maggie to develop feelings for one another. But if we were going to handpick someone for him, we couldn't find anyone more perfect than your daughter. You raised an amazing young woman that we have loved forever. And as strange as all of this seems, the more we think about it..."

"The more it makes sense," Matthew and Janice said together.

"Dexter," Lenore said as she rose from the table. "I know you love Maggie, but you've given that child some hard years."

"I've done everything I could for that girl..." Dexter interrupted.

Lenore turned to face her husband. "Everything but accept her for who she is."

Dexter raised his index finger to make a pointed

protest, but Lenore would not be deterred. "No, old man," she said as she approached him. "You and Maggie have gone around and around about the kind of career she should have, the man she should marry...even the size she should be."

"Lennie," Dexter said, invoking a rarely-used nickname. "I just wanted her to be happy."

"As happy as she was with Richard?"

"But Richard..."

"But Richard what? That girl went through years of misery...*years!* Sacrificing her own happiness and self worth to be in a Dexter-approved relationship. She was miserable! And when she tried to strike out on her own, he humiliated her. And you supported *him*! No wonder she hardly ever comes home. Why should she, when the one place she feels accepted and loved is in Joe Buchannan's house?"

Silence ruled the room for an indeterminate amount of time before Janice stepped in to assist her friend's argument. "Maggie didn't fall for Joe because he represented some sort of life she wanted..."

"She fell for Joe because he gave her what she needed." Lenore said. "Peace of mind. Shame on you for not being able to see that for your own child."

Just then, a rare occurrence: Dexter made a startling admission as he sank back down on the couch.

"I...I am sorry. I was wrong."

A collective sigh emanated from everyone in the room.

"So let's just talk to Joe, and Maggie, okay?" Lenore said. "We need to let them know that we're on their side."

"That's good to know."

The four adults turned to see Joe standing in the doorway.

"Hey, son," Matthew said. "Come on in. We wanna talk to you."

Joe entered the room with a great deal of trepidation. Not entirely sure of Dexter's feelings, he created a safe distance from him on the opposite side of the room.

"Mr. West," Joe began.

Dexter held up his hands to stop him. "Son, it's okay. We've been talking to Maggie from the road. She's really happy with her appearances and concerts. We could tell, however that something was missing."

"Turns out, that something was you," Lenore added.

"I don't even know if I have a shot with her now," Joe said. "It feels like her life is taking off, and she's leaving the rest of us behind."

Dexter rose from his place on the sofa, walked over to Joe and extended his hand. Joe stood and shook it.

"There's only one way to find out," Dexter said.

Chapter 14

"Okay troops, time to eat," Joe said as he scooped potato salad onto paper plates. The warm spring evening was practically an engraved invitation for a barbecue. With Matthew and Dexter at the grill, and their wives readying the side dishes on the West's patio, all that was left to do was corral the children who were playing in the back yard.

Stumbling over one another like puppies, the twins elbowed their way to their tables, while Gwen took her usual place as far away from them as possible.

As burgers and hot dogs were distributed and grace was said over the meal, Joe and Matthew locked eyes; the latter nodding as if to say, *Now's the time.*

"Hey gang, we wanna talk with you about something," Joe said, taking advantage of the rare moment of peace that occurred when the children's mouths were full. He looked at Gwen, who knew immediately what the topic was going to be. She stopped just short of taking a bite of her sandwich to smile at her father. Joe returned her look with one of his own.

"Wassup, Daddy?" Matty said, his mouth full of half chewed burger.

The table was silent for a moment as Joe girded up his resolve. He cleared his throat before starting. "Well, I wanted to talk to you about Aunt Maggie."

"When's she coming home?" Mary Margaret asked.

"You miss her, huh?" was Joe's response.

"Sure do," said Matty, finally swallowing his food. "You miss her too, Dad?"

"Yes. Yes I do. How would you feel about her coming to stay with us?"

Mary Margaret's face brightened considerably. "You mean like forever?"

"Yeah."

"Like a...*mom*, forever?"

Joe and the other adults exchanged looks of astonishment. "I can't get anything past you guys, can I?"

"Nope," said Matty, his face awash in potato salad, only partially aware of what was going on.

"Anyway," Janice said as she wiped her grandson's mouth clean, "I think what your dad is trying to say..."

"...what I'm trying to say is that I think I want to...m-marry her and have her come to live with us."

The twins ceased their activity. First looking at one another, they then turned to face their sister. Gwen's eyes were still bolted on her father's; her smile still securely in place.

She nodded ever so slightly, urging him on.

"What would you think about that?"

"I think it would be awesome," said Mary Margaret instantly.

Matty seemed more circumspect. Deeply considering the question as he began to take another bite of burger, he stopped and asked, "Wait...if Aunt Maggie becomes our new mom...does that mean that *they* aren't my grandma and grandpa anymore?" pointing at the Hammonds.

"No," all the adults said together. "Absolutely not!"

"We'll always be Grandma and Grandpa," Matthew said.

"But now, you will be the most blessed little children in the world, because..." Lenore began.

"Because you will have *three* sets of grandparents," Dexter said. Still looking at the children, Lenore smiled with genuine affection and took her husband's hand.

Matty carefully considered this new arrangement. As if his approval was what stood between Joe and his future, the entire table rested their gaze on the boy. His concentration evident, he placed the rest of his burger on his plate. "Grandma and Grandpa West," he said quietly, as if trying it on for size.

"How does that sound?"

"I like it," he said definitively. "More grandparents, more presents on my birthday!" he said, shrugging his shoulders as if this were the only logical conclusion.

Everyone at the table laughed aloud. Everyone except Joe, who simply smiled sweetly at his precocious offspring, praying silently that he could convince Maggie just as easily.

Chapter 15

W hile a song played on her car radio, Sissy's conversation with her mother played in her head. It started as innocently as any other call. But as Janice began to broach the subject of Joe and the children, Sissy realized this wasn't going to be an easy, lighthearted exchange.

"Sissy…" Janice drew out her name slowly.

"What, Mother?"

"What is it you think you're doing?

"Again, Mother, I have no idea to what you are referring." Sissy's tone was clipped and defensive.

"I think you do."

After several seconds of silence, Janice continued. "Just stop this, honey. Please. Joe is not a prize to be won, and Maggie is not the enemy."

Sissy had taken all that she could. Like a dam beginning to burst, she could feel a pressure rise within her.

"But she just swept liked she owned the place," Sissy complained. "Sh-she just came in and took over - the kids, the house, Joe…"

"Oh Sis, she did not and you know it."

"She practically commandeered Gracie's funeral arrangements…even decided what Grace would be buried in!"

"Sissy, she was the only one who had the presence of mind to make those decisions during that time. We were a mess, and Maggie was Grace's best friend..."

"But this is *my* family...and she has *no right...*" Sissy spat. Her breathing was shallow and rapid. Her free hand was balled into a fist, softly pounding into the center of her chest. "This was *mine*...not hers!"

"Sissy, do you even hear yourself? What is happening to you? What are you even talking about?"

"Why are you sticking up for her? Don't you see she's invaded our lives? With her boyfriend drama and her fat issues...ugh! All her little goody-goody ways... *'Please Mom Hammond, let me help you with this. Here, Dad Hammond, I'll take care of that. Oh kids, I'll feed you and help you with your homework.'* You couldn't see it, but I could!"

Sissy's tenor was brutal and mocking, and from Janice's perspective, completely unhinged.

"All of that was a front, Mother. Her only goal was to become the next Mrs. Joe Buchanan!"

Janice was dumbfounded. "Sissy," was all she could say.

"There is no way that Nashville society would accept them as a couple. I don't care what year it is, or how far we've supposedly come; she's *completely unworthy* of him! Can you actually tell me you can see Joe walking into a society function with a woman who is little more than his big ol' maid?"

The heart of the matter was beginning to surface, and it made Janice sick. "Sissy! I do not believe this is coming from you. I did not raise my child to speak like this. Stop. stop it, now!"

But Sissy couldn't stop. "Why do you think I worked so to get her out on the road? I don't care about her or her lousy singing career. I needed to get her away from Joe. With her out of the picture, he was able to see *me*! I needed a chance for him to see me…to see me as something other than…"

"His sister?"

Those two words stopped Sissy cold. She caught a glimpse of herself in the mirror. Her face was flushed. She barely recognized herself.

"But I'm not his sister," she said quietly.

"To him, sweetheart, you *are*," Janice said with compassion. "But Joe and the children are not a birthright for you to inherit."

Sissy began to protest, but Janice continued. "Honey, you left town the second you were old enough. And Maggie took her place in Grace's life because it's what was meant to happen. Grace, Joe and the kids - they were her world. Then when Gracie left us, well, Maggie didn't set out to be the next Mrs. Buchanan, that's for sure. I would bet my life on that. But she truly cared for all of us. That care came from genuine concern. And from that concern grew a friendship. And from that friendship came the sisterhood that existed between Maggie and Grace. Nothing was forced then, and nothing's being forced now."

Sissy slowly sat down on her sofa. "I remember the first time Gracie brought him home. He was sweet and kind. So attentive…"

"And he was completely in love with Grace. Honey, he's exceedingly handsome; and more important, he's a good man with a sweet nature. That's why everyone loves him."

"But *I* love him mom…"

"No, sweetie, you don't. You love the life you think you're supposed to have with him. You thought that this would be some seamless transition to which you were entitled. But you can't force yourself into this situation by badmouthing Maggie or going to extremes to get her out of the way. You and Joe? It's totally wrong, and you know it."

Janice could hear her daughter begin to cry softly. "Oh Sis," she said. "I'm so sorry that you're hurting. I'm sorry that you are lonely. But trying to take Grace's place isn't the way to banish those feelings."

Sissy curled herself into the corner of her sofa and cried a little harder.

"I know you feel as though everything came easier for Grace. But I'm going to tell you something you might find hard to believe," Janice said.

"Okay, what?" Sissy said, sniffing.

"Grace was often jealous of you."

"I don't believe you."

"It's true. Your talents took you around the world; she had to hold down the fort with her family. And while she loved being a wife and mother, you've got to know that watching the world evolve around her was agony."

"We talked all the time, but she never said anything close to that."

"Why would she? She knew that she was where she was meant to be, sweetie. She loved her husband and her kids with everything that was in her, and her job was to get them on their way. Despite her disappointment over some unfulfilled dreams, well…Grace took charge of her life, and she adjusted her story. Or at least she started to…" Janice's voice trailed off at the reality of Grace's passing.

"And on top of everything else, she's not here anymore. But you are. Celebrate all that you were created to be, and stop settling for something just because it looks good on the surface. So your life isn't what you had planned. Take some time to adjust *your* story; really think about what *you* want and need; not how you can be a continuation of your sister's life."

Janice prayed that her words had taken root before attempting to lighten the air. "Hey, little girl," she said cheerfully. "Let's get a silver lining going here."

Sissy scoffed as she wiped away her tears. "Oh I can't wait to hear this," she said.

"Look at the life you've created for yourself," Janice said. "You're young, you're beautiful, and you're smart and accomplished. What man wouldn't be interested in that?"

"Oh mom..."

"Don't 'oh mom' me. You probably have several dozen guys chomping at the bit to take you out, but you've been so single-minded in your devotion to Joe, you didn't even know any of them were alive."

Sissy took a moment to consider the idea. "I feel so lost. I don't know what to do."

"Yes you do, honey. Live your life. Follow your path. I would bet my life on this too..."

"You are playing fast and loose with your life with all this betting, you know," said Sissy, trying to lighten things for herself.

Janice chuckled. "Okay, not so much with the betting. More like, I have faith; faith that the God who created you with all these gifts, talents and abilities, didn't do it for you to take on this world alone. He's got someone for you - someone far more perfect than you could ever contrive for yourself. And in the end, you'll be at peace."

The song on the radio came to an end. Sissy turned off the car and gripped the steering wheel with both hands. Leaning forward, she rested her forehead on it and exhaled simultaneously.

After a moment's contemplation, she checked her reflection in the mirror, smoothed a tear-smudged portion of mascara under her eye, and exited her car. As she walked up the footpath to Joe's back door, she took a deep breath and did something she'd never done in all the years she'd visited his house.

She knocked.

"Sissy." Joe said with a look of bewilderment. "Did you lose your key?"

He leaned on the frame of the doorway, a dish towel over his shoulder. Somewhere in the distance, a small smack could be heard. "Mary Margaret!" he yelled over his shoulder. Quickly turning his attention to Sissy, he motioned for her to enter. "Sorry, hon, come on in."

Sissy sheepishly entered the door as Mary Margaret made her way to the kitchen. With a look of utter innocence she asked, "What's up, Daddy?"

"What's up, darling daughter of mine, is that slap I just heard. What did I tell you about slapping your brother?"

Mary Margaret took a moment to ponder the question. "It's not good?"

Joe's eyes widened in amazement at her response. "No, it's not good." He turned to look at Sissy with an expression that said, "Are you kidding me?"

Sissy's response was a tentative smile. She could remember a time not so long ago, when being at the center of a domestic moment like this was exactly where she wanted to be.

"Please go to your room," Joe said. "I will deal with you later."

"But Dad, he started it!"

"He usually does, but it's always the second kid - namely you - who gets caught. I'll take care of him, but you, off to the room, now!"

Frustrated, Mary Margaret slowly ascended the stairs. "Sissy, please let me take your coat, I'm so sorry," Joe said, heading toward the doorway that lead out of the kitchen to the rest of the house. "As you can see, it's just another night at the zoo. If you could give me a minute and let me punish my children, I promise you'll have my undivided attention. Matty!" he shouted around the corner.

"Joe, wait," Sissy said, touching him lightly on the arm before immediately pulling it away. Joe stopped momentarily as Matty entered the room. Holding him firmly by the shoulder, Joe looked at Sissy and asked, "Sis, what's wrong?"

Hoping for a reprieve from obvious punishment, Matty looked up at his father. "Room. Now." Joe said, dashing that hope almost instantly. Without argument, Matty made his way to his room.

Sissy retrieved her keys and an envelope from her purse. Removing the key that belonged to the Buchanan home, she placed it on the table. "Here," she said, pushing both the key and the envelope slightly toward him.

Distracted by this latest drama with the twins, Joe was confused. "What on earth is all this?"

Sissy cleared her throat. "Well, I...I um, wanted to say that I was sorry for all of the trouble I caused."

"Okay," Joe said. "But giving back the house key? That's a bit extreme."

"Maybe. But I think I need to be. I just wanted you to know that I wouldn't be stopping by anymore."

"Sis, let's find a happy medium here. Come, sit."

Taking a seat at the kitchen table, she refused when Joe offered her something to drink. "I just wanted to say…um…I need to tell you something." She gave a nervous laugh as she said, "Maybe I will have a glass of water."

Joe poured the glass and brought it to her as he joined her at the kitchen table. He leaned forward and braced himself for whatever Sissy had to say. As a tear rested just above her lower lash, she took a sip of water, and made her confession.

"The morning, after…um, the um…." She began, unable to define her embarrassing encounter in Joe's bedroom that night.

"Let's just call it, *the incident*," Joe broke in.

"Fine. The morning after *the incident*, when we were here in the kitchen…"

Joe's brow furrowed in concentration. "Yeah…"

"Maggie was at the door. Your back was to her, so you couldn't see her…but I did."

Joe leaned back in his chair, mortified. "You were in my robe," he said quietly.

"Yes," Sissy replied. "And then…I…I borrowed…um, I mean I took…a shirt from your closet. The green one."

"Yeah, I wondered where that went. My mom bought me that shirt."

"I know. It's why I took it. Anyway, I wore it to Maggie's session later that day. On purpose."

The revelation left Joe completely thrown. "Sissy," he whispered. "How could you?"

He began to rise from the table. He had no idea who this woman was that was before him and wasn't sure if he wanted to be anywhere near her. Sissy reached out in an attempt to persuade him not to bolt from the room. "Joe, please," she pleaded. "Hear me out. I know I was wrong, and I want to make amends."

Joe did not return to his seat; instead, he chose to lean against the counter to hear what she had to say.

"I am the reason that Maggie never called. I made it my purpose to keep you two as far away as possible: The radio tour, getting her on any and every conceivable opening slot for every artist we had out there. I wasn't doing it just to be kind or to give her career a boost…"

"Then why?"

"You know why," she said wearily. "I've been in love with you from the day Grace brought you home. And Maggie, to my way of thinking, was always in the way."

Joe tilted his head back and squeezed his eyes shut. Pinching the bridge of his nose, he said, "I don't know what to say."

"There is nothing for you to say, Joe. This is me. This is all on me. I've been completely deluding myself into thinking that this was something that was meant to be. So when I heard about Blake and Maggie's little rendezvous at the studio…"

Joe had hoisted himself onto the counter and placed his forearms on his knees. "Ah, you heard about that, huh?"

"Oh, everybody did. How did you hear about it?"

"I went to the studio to see Maggie and take her out to celebrate her last day of recording."

"And you actually saw them there."

"Yep."

"I guess my telling you what kind of a womanizer he was didn't help."

"No, not really."

Sissy twisted a tissue in her hands as she continued. "So, anyway, when I heard about that little interlude they shared, I felt like it was all coming together. Blake would take Maggie away, and it would be clear for you and me. But there was one thing I didn't count on."

"What was that?"

Sissy moved a hand through her hair to pull it away from her face. The strawberry blonde tresses swept back into place almost immediately.

"The truth," she said through slow-falling tears. "The truth of it all is that, no matter what I tried to say, or do, I didn't fit. Not the way Maggie does. She makes your heart happy. She brings joy to the children."

"They really miss her. She calls Gwennie all the time, even chats with the twins. I'm told she asks about me, but I've not spoken to her since..."

"Since the day I made her think..."Sissy broke in.

"Yeah," Joe said.

"Joe I am so sorry. If I could take it all back, I promise you, I would."

"I believe that. Thank you."

Sissy drew in a deep breath in relief. "If it means anything, I really don't believe Maggie is lost to you. That dinner between the two of them? It was just that - a dinner."

Joe nodded, but said nothing.

So," she said, placing her hand on the key. "Giving you guys a much needed break from me, is my attempt to make it up to you."

Joe hopped down from the counter and picked up the key. Opening up her hand, he placed the key on her palm.

"Sissy," he said as he took the seat next to her. "You don't have go away completely. You're my sis..."

He stopped short, not wanting to compound her hurt with that word. "We're family. And family is always supposed to stay connected." He wrapped her fingers around the key and closed her hand in both of his.

"With boundaries." He said with a grin. They laughed.

Joe finally acknowledged the envelope. "Oh, yeah, what's this?"

Sissy dabbed at her eyes with the tissue and said cheerfully, "Open it. It's for you."

The business sized envelope was thicker than just a plain piece of paper. Inside there was a ticket and a laminated pass on a lanyard. Both had the same beautifully shot photo of Maggie prominently featured on the front, with information about the showcase printed on the back.

"The show's in two hours," she said.

Joe was surprised. "Sis…are you sure?"

"Absolutely." She gestured towards the stairs. "So, you'd better get going. Your hair alone takes an hour."

Joe beamed. "Gwennie," he called. He knew she was in the living room, but she didn't answer.

He found her on the couch listening to music on her cell while working on a book report. Joe shook his head in irritation as he removed her headphones. "We're not even going to get into how this little scenario isn't helping you get your school work done effectively." Gwen returned his look of annoyance, but said nothing. "How old are you now? Eighteen? Nineteen?" he asked.

She rolled her eyes. "I'm fourteen Dad, you know that."

"Okay, fourteen. Ready for your first babysitting gig?"

Gwen closed her laptop and bounded onto the sofa with excitement. "Really? Am I gonna get paid?"

"Off the couch, Tom Cruise," he said. "Yeah, I'll pay ya. Five bucks an hour."

"Awesome!"

"One rule," Matty and M&M are in eternal time out. They're not allowed out of their rooms tonight except to go to the bathroom."

Gwen dramatically clasped her hands together and feigned swooning. "Oh, Thank you Lord!" she cried. "It's a freakin' miracle! A dream come true!"

"Okay, whatever, but you're dealing with children who know how to break into things, so be on your guard, got it?"

Gwen stood at attention and gave him a salute. "Got it. Where are you going anyway?"

"To see Aunt Maggie."

Gwen's face took on a radiance as she smiled. "Well alright," she said, nodding.

Joe made his way over to Sissy. "Thanks again, Sis."

"No problem," she said with a genuine smile.

"Hey, are you gonna go? This is a big night for everyone involved, and that would include you, right?"

"I think I'll sit tonight out, but you need to get going. Have a great time."

"Aunt Sissy," Gwen called from the couch. "You wanna hang out and have some pizza?"

Sissy looked at Joe, who heard the question and stopped on the landing of the stairs. He smiled, nodded, and mouthed the words, "Go ahead."

"Sure, Gwennie," Sissy said. "I'll get the menu."

Chapter 16

I t was Lanie's idea to hold Maggie's showcase at The Factory. The historic site on the north end of Franklin had long been not only a premier collection of art galleries, fine dining and high-end shopping boutiques; it had also expanded its reputation as a top entertainment venue.

She was painstakingly thorough in her attempt to transform one of facility's many halls into a chic, intimate setting. Gauzy white drapery was hung from floor to ceiling around the perimeter of the room. Hundreds of string lights were placed behind the fabric to give the room a warm glow. Antique chandeliers hung from the ceiling, and there were flowers and greenery throughout the room.

Onstage, there were Persian-style rugs on the floor as well as the backdrop behind the band. Candelabras decorated the landscape; barstools were covered with black velvet to give the seats a lux look. In the center of the stage was black baby grand piano with Maggie's logo beautifully etched on the side.

Despite the rich, captivating surroundings, it was that final feature that fascinated Joe the most. He stared entranced at her name and raised his hand to the side of the instrument, brushing his fingertips against it.

"Don't touch that, please," came a voice from behind

him. Startled, he whipped around quickly and apologized to a facility staff member. It was then that he noticed the stage, light and television crews, testing their cameras, microphones and various cables. Joe knew he was in the way.

"Could you direct me to the green room," he asked the staff member, flashing his laminate.

Winding his way through the makeshift backstage area, a familiar tension found its way to Joe's chest. He was nervous. The tension was dispelled, however, at the sight of Lenore West.

"Joe honey, is that you?" she said, making her way toward him.

"Lenore, so good to see you," he replied.

As they embraced, she pushed him out at arms' length to look at him. Beaming, she said, "I am so happy you're here."

Joe returned her smile with one of his own. "You too. But will she be?"

"Yes. Yes she will," Lenore said definitively. "She's in her dressing room right now. Her dad couldn't come because of a trial he's presiding over; so when I stepped out, she was on the phone with him."

"Oh, sorry the Judge couldn't make it," he said.

"I know. He was heartbroken, but Maggie understood. Actually, I've gotta scoot. They've forgotten her club sodas, so I've been sent on an errand."

"Ah, well, I'm just going to pace back and forth out here out of sheer terror, if it's all the same to you."

Lenore gave him a playful slap on the arm as the two of them laughed. "Seriously, I think I'll wait to talk to her. I don't want to mess up her pre-game," said Joe.

"Suit yourself," she said. "But I have it on good

authority, she'll be happy to see you."

"Thank you, mom." Joe kissed her gently on the cheek.

"Mom. I like the sound of that. Keep that up." She smiled at him and began to turn to complete her assignment. Her way, however, was momentarily blocked by a tall blonde man who had been striding confidently toward them.

"G'day," Blake said; his Aussie magnetism on full throttle as he took her hand. "You *must* be Maggie West's sister." It took everything within Joe not to roll his eyes.

"Ha!" Lenore exclaimed, fully aware of the fact that this young man was attempting to charm her. "No, I'm her mother," she said with skeptically raised eyebrow.

Blake kissed her hand as he introduced himself. "Blake Fabian, at your service, Mrs. West. I like to think of myself as the architect of The Maggie West Sound."

Lenore's eyes completely betrayed the smile that was fixed on her face. She was nobody's fool, and she knew a snow job when she encountered one.

"I've always been of the understanding that God Himself was the architect of The Maggie West Sound," she said icily as she slowly pulled her hand out of Blake's.

Joe shielded his expression by turning away and running his hand through his hair. "Wow," he mouthed in amazement.

"Yes ma'am," Blake said quickly and respectfully. "Can't argue with that." Nervously, he cleared his throat and nodded in her direction. "It was indeed an honor."

"Yes, nice to meet you as well. Thank you for helping my daughter realize her dream," she said with a bit more kindness. "If you gentlemen will excuse me, I need to see about something for Maggie. Young man?" she said, directing her attention to Joe.

"Ma'am?"

Her response was simply a wink and a smile as she walked away.

Joe smiled after her as Blake quietly said, "You're gonna have to give me your secret."

"I'm sorry?"

"How to charm a woman in the West family," Blake said with jocularity. "She's as tough as her daughter."

"The one thing I've learned about the women in the West family," Joe said as he backed his way toward a coffee machine, "is that they are women of a singular devotion. They know who they love, and they don't stray from it."

"Well, that certainly seems to be true." Just then, Blake's face took on a look of recognition. "You're Joe, right?"

It was at that moment that Joe realized for all the times he'd been in the studio to see Maggie work, this was the first time her producer actually acknowledged his presence. "I'm Blake," he went on. "How ya goin' mate?"

"I'm...goin' fine, thanks," Joe said cautiously, unfamiliar with Blake's colloquialism. "Coffee?" he offered.

"Yeah, thanks."

"Now Mag, that is a killer outfit."

Maggie had to agree. Tessa, her stylist, crafted a look that was fashion forward, while age appropriate. The caramel colored suede top gave her skin a fresh glow, and the beveled fringe that hung from the neckline to the bottom hem complemented her shape. Dark green khakis with high heeled brown suede boots complete the organic, bohemian ensemble. Her makeup was fresh and clean, her jewelry minimal, and her curls were soft, simple and uncomplicated.

"You look like a rock star, lady," Lanie said with pride.

"She *is* a rock star," Tessa added.

Maggie looked at herself from every angle. "It does work, doesn't it?"

"Have I ever steered you wrong," asked Tessa.

"Not ever, my dear," Maggie said sweetly. "Not ever."

Lenore entered the room, along with Darla and a woman carrying a tray with bottles of mineral water and glasses full of ice. The crescendo of noise from the hallway quickly abated as she shut the door.

"My goodness," Lenore said. "It's turning into a real circus out there, honey!"

"And it's all for you," Lanie said as she placed her hands on Maggie's shoulders. "Are you ready? It's just about show time."

Maggie nodded, her stomach in knots. Breaking away to accept the glass her mother poured, she sipped slowly, closed her eyes, and swallowed.

"How you doin' Sugar?" Darla asked. "Nervous?"

In truth, Maggie was terrified. She could see the night at the arena with Deana, and remembered the intimidation her former boss had felt bringing her show back home. She chastised herself for her mocking of Deana and feeling as though her behavior was over the top and dramatic.

Just then, her mind returned to Grace. Briefly, she remembered that the night of that same Arena concert was the night Grace had her accident, but her thoughts were more centered on how this moment just didn't feel right without her. Or the kids. Or Joe.

Suddenly, a wave rushed over her. For the time since

this odyssey began, she was able to separate her desire for Joe from her loyalty to Grace. It fascinated her, and in a strange way, made her miss them both all the more.

"She'd be proud of you honey," Lenore said softly so that only she could hear. "In some small way, Grace is watching out for you. So you do your best for her too, okay?"

Her mother's insanely accurate intuition nearly brought Maggie to tears. Gripping her hand, Maggie's eyes misted, but she didn't cry. "Thanks mom."

"Okay," Lanie began, shifting into business mode. "The camera crew is outside. We're going to have you and your mom come out, we'll get you to the stage, and boom…the magic will begin."

"No. Mom should get to her seat," Maggie protested.

"We'll take care of your mother," Lanie said with a motherly tone of her own. "It'll be great for the start of the taping for everyone to see your number one fan walking with you by your side."

As the dressing room door opened, cameras flashed furiously. Lenore was briefly startled by all of the activity, and wished she'd been shown to her seat. She marveled at her daughter's calm, and squeezed her hand.

Shouts of congratulations, well wishes and general applause filled the air as the entourage made their way to the stage. Maggie was gracious, stopping periodically to shake hands and hug people; introducing her mother along the way.

Joe shook Blake's hand; a fitting benediction to what turned out to be an intriguing and informative conversation about the heart of Maggie West.

Glancing at his cell phone, Blake said, "Well, it sounds

like things are getting underway. It was great to meet you Joe. Good luck tonight."

"I should be wishing you luck," Joe said. "You put a lot of work into this thing."

"Thanks. It was a pleasure. But I'm thinking the real music will be made *after* the show," he said with a sly grin.

Joe laughed. "From your mouth to God's ears," he said as he neared the doorway. Turning to exit, he found himself directly in Maggie's path.

For a moment, they both stood transfixed; neither of them saying a word. Camera shutters continued to click, flashes popped. The bewildered crowd quieted, and entertainment reporters craned their necks. Maggie West had yet to be linked romantically with anyone, and now everyone was wondering just who this mystery man might be.

"You came," Maggie said. The light in her eyes was impossible to hide.

"I wouldn't have missed this for the world," Joe replied.

"Maggie," a reporter shouted. "Is that your boyfriend?"

She turned in the direction of the media. Cameras of all forms continued to capture the moment, including that of the crew from CMT. Whispering to the segment director, a man holding a bulky camera on his shoulder asked, "Are we supposed to be recording this?"

"Absolutely," Lanie whispered from behind them. "Do not stop rolling."

In the crush of the crowd, no one could see Joe take Maggie's hand in his. "Knock 'em dead, kiddo," he whispered out of the side of his mouth.

Still silent, a slow, somewhat enigmatic smile swept across Maggie's face. Relishing her newfound power,

Maggie simply said, "Enjoy the show, everyone."

Maggie stood in the center of the empty platform. In the silence of the now vacated hall, she could feel everything: The beat of the music, the love of the crowd, the emotions that flowed from her to the audience and back during the four-minute standing ovation. Drawing in a breath, she closed her eyes and savored every second.

From the moment she took the stage, Maggie was in command. Gracious and fun with her veteran guests, solid when she sang solo; even conducting a choir, there wasn't a moment where she was not completely at the top of her game.

The soft whir of a vacuum purred in the distance, while the cleaning crews stacked chairs, dismantled tables, and bagged trash. Gone were the flowers and fancy decorations; the lights, the cameras, the microphones, even her beautiful Steinway baby grand. Standing beneath a solitary light, Maggie marveled at how quickly everything could be taken down and put away after such a meticulous set up.

Grace returned to her memory. That was most certainly a meticulous set up. Years and years of friendship; laughter, tears, good times - and the occasional spat over something silly and unimportant. A good life with her best friend...taken down and quickly put away by one drunk driver.

She considered the career that waited before her. The dive bars, the seemingly endless road trips and tours, stingy club owners who paid her less than what she was worth; flaky musicians who would cancel on her at the last minute. They were all part of the meticulous set up. But like many of her peers and heroes before her, one failed album, one bad business decision, one substance abuse problem could cause a career to be taken down and quickly put away.

All her life, she'd allowed others to define her. She didn't mind being known as Grace's best friend. She stayed with Richard because she didn't feel as though anyone else would have her. She settled for a role in the background because of a handful of opinions that said that was where she belonged.

But right now, in this moment, Maggie West began to understand, that those things were all part of the ultimate set up. The ache of missing Grace would never fully subside, and she'd miss the camaraderie of the Timmons band, but coursing through her veins was a new power, a new resolve. She'd survived the damaging, juvenile relationship she had with Richard. She could make it. She would make it. She proved it to Nashville, and now Maggie West was ready to take on the world. Until tonight however, she was prepared to do it all on her own.

But Joe was there. He had come. She didn't have to beg. She'd been brave enough to actually let that dream go. And there he was, of his own volition.

She looked at the spot on the floor where his chair had been. Where he sat with pride in his eyes and a smile on his perfect lips, shedding a tear during the song she'd written about Grace; spellbound when he heard the finished version of the song she'd written for him, clapping along to the pounding rhythms of the triumphant gospel-choir finale. Cheering for her, perhaps louder than anyone in the audience.

Maggie flexed the fingers on the hand he'd held

backstage, remembering how his strength intertwined with hers. As she brought her hands up to her face, she promised herself that if given the chance, she would pour more of herself into every set up, lest it all be taken down and quickly put away.

Suddenly, a voice cut through the darkness.

"Share your life with me, Maggie."

Maggie turned to see Joe emerge from the shadows.

"Where have you been?"

"I've been laying low. Thought I'd spare us both the press attention."

Maggie walked toward him. "Well, you've become media savvy all of a sudden," she quipped.

"Hey, you're getting us off the subject," Joe said.

"And that was?"

"Your life," Joe said, suddenly serious. "You have an amazing, spectacular life. You bring light into every room you enter, and you make my crazy world so peaceful." He reached up and touched her face. "Your beauty comes from the inside out. It always has."

Joe narrowed his gaze and looked at Maggie with a directness that made her knees give way. "I am so sorry for everything. The misunderstandings, the distance between us, for being the big ol' wimp that I am."

Maggie began to speak, but Joe gently placed a finger on her lips. "Shh. Let me finish. You've been on your way for quite some time, kid. But you can't do this alone. You need backup from the folks you love, and from the folks who love you."

Maggie's eyes widened as Joe got down on one knee. "I am one of those folks. *I* love you."

Laughter came through the tears that had begun to spring from Maggie's eyes as Joe went on.

"You, Mary Margaret West, have become the love of my life. I don't ever want to let you down again. In the time we've been apart, I have learned one very important truth: I am at my best when I am with you, and I don't function at all without you."

"Umm…That's actually *two* important truths," she cracked.

"Smart-aleck," he said, grimacing. "You've always kept me on my toes. I wanna keep it that way. So, I'm gonna say it again. Share your life with me."

The room had come to a standstill. The cleaning crew had taken notice of the exchange and ceased their activity. Lenore and Darla hid in a darkened doorway, clutching hands in anticipation.

"Okay, you're killing me here, West," Joe pleaded as she remained silent. "That's the best proposal I've got."

Slowly, Maggie got down on her own knee and laced her fingers through his. "That's the only proposal I need," she said. "I love you too."

Chapter 17

The headline read: *Grammy-Winning Songstress to Wed University Scholar in Lavish Star-Studded Affair at Ryman Auditorium.*

"Who knew you were a scholar?" Declan joked as he dropped the newspaper in front of Joe.

Finishing his coffee, Joe chuckled. "Just one of my many, many talents," he said.

Declan was unimpressed. "Okay, Mr. Multi-talent, time to suit up," he said as he handed Joe his tuxedo.

"Well, this has been quite a year," Declan went on as he poured his own coffee down the sink. "Does it feel weird?"

"You mean the fact that you're my best man? Again?"

"Well, yeah…that. And exactly who it is you are marrying."

Joe contemplated the question for a moment. "No. I mean, I can see how it could be strange," he said.

"I hate to say it, but this is a double dose of strange in my book."

Declan's statement caught Joe off guard. "Please don't tell me, today of all days, that you're bugged by this. Because after everything we've been through to get here…"

"No. *No!*" Declan broke in, trying to form the correct thought. "It's just kinda strange that you're marrying…that I'm friends with…you know…*the* Maggie West. I mean, she's become this serious *celebrity*. And you are the one who gets to marry her. It's just strange, man."

Joe had to laugh out loud. "*That's* what you're thinking about? That's she's famous now?"

Declan blushed in embarrassment at his adolescent thoughts. "Well, she's always just been, *Maggie*. Now she's *Maggie West*. I'm seeing our friend on magazines and red carpets - with your ugly mug. Yeah, that's what's bugging me. It's ticking me off that you married up, *twice*."

Joe smirked. "Don't tell me you're contemplating the end of your bachelorhood."

"I dunno. I mean, I'm not getting any younger."

"You've not seen the guest list."

Joe had Declan's full attention. "Really? Who's coming?"

Joe scratched his chin. "Welllll…" he said, drawing out the word. "I'm pretty sure I saw the name of that action movie actress…Haley…um, Haley…"

"Haley Heath?"

"Yeah, that's it. Haley Heath."

"You've got to be kidding me. You guys know *Haley Heath*? Haley 'hotter than Angelina' Heath?"

"Well, Maggie does. They met out in LA. You know, you're starting to sound like Gwen when she's talking about that kid in that boy band. And you've got a little drool…"

"Shut up," Declan said. He gave Joe a playful shove. "Anyway," he said, "despite the fact that you're getting ready to marry another amazing woman, seriously, I'm really happy for you man."

"Thanks."

"Now get upstairs and get it together. This is a little too touchy-feely for me, and it's making me uncomfortable."

"Awwww...c'mere, you," Joe teased. He grabbed Declan and gave him an overly affectionate hug.

"Ugh! Stop it man, seriously," Declan complained as he wrestled him off. "You *will* show up at your wedding with a busted jaw, I promise."

The Ryman was Deana's idea. She recalled attending the wedding of another artist friend a few years back. So as only the Queen of Nashville could, she wielded her power and influence and secured the venue; primarily out of love for her former employee. But in her heart of hearts, Deana knew her husband's manipulations to keep Maggie in their camp were more than she could bear. The Ryman was more than Deana's wedding gift: it was her penance.

Lenore and Tessa, stylist turned wedding coordinator, were busy directing traffic; telling delivery men if flowers should go in the auditorium or to the reception hall around the corner. Darla, Chrissy Boyd, and the rest of the bridesmaids were in dressing rooms, putting on their finishing touches.

Seated in one of the busier rooms, Mary Margaret watched the preparation with a sense of awe and wonder, as if she'd landed in some mystical world of life-sized Barbie dolls. Fully dressed and ready to carry out her duties as the flower girl, she held her basket gently, yet firmly, guarded like a priceless treasure.

Gwen sat next to her; a junior bridesmaid - dressed and ready as well. She reached into her purse and pulled out her phone when she felt the vibration. She'd just received a text...from Sissy.

Gwen felt a slight wave of awkwardness come over

her. While Sissy had taken a low profile in the past year, getting a text from her on this particular day felt a bit ominous. After a quick mental tussle, the teen figured that no matter what it said, she didn't have to share it with anyone, so she chose to read it.

Hey there sweet pea...just wanted to wish everyone well.

Gwen looked at the message with a sad smile. She knew this was hard for her aunt, and appreciated the gesture. Just then, another text from Sissy came through.

Also wanted to give you a look at what's been keeping me busy lately ;)

The message was followed by a picture of Sissy, playfully enveloped by a handsome, tanned, rugged-type man. The expression on both of their faces could only be described as pure joy. Their attire suggested that they were at a party of some sort, surrounded by other equally joyful friends.

Wow, Aunt Sis, that's a great picture!

I know, right???? I think we're gonna make it official!

You're getting married?

LOL...no, well...not yet. We're officially a 'couple', though!

I liked him when you brought him to the house a few months back...what's his name again?

Mark Kirby.

Well, I like him!

Me too! ☺ call you tomorrow!

k...bye!

"Gwennie, sugar," Darla said, breaking Gwen's concentration. Have you seen Maggie? Her dressing room is empty."

Someone handed Lenore a brilliantly wrapped silver box. On the card was an inscription:

Joe and Maggie...Wishing you God's best on this blessed day. The mixture of emotions is difficult to sort out, but we know one thing...we are truly thankful that the two of you found one another. Now you are REALLY family, Maggie...we love you so much. We are with you in spirit, enjoying the celebration!
Love,
Janice and Matt

Lenore misted ever so slightly at the beautifully written note. She couldn't even begin to fathom what her friends were going through on this day. Still, it was a kind thing to do, and she knew Maggie and Joe would feel the Hammond's blessing.

Bustling down the stairs, Gwen, Mary Margaret, and Darla interrupted Lenore's train of thought. Talking over one another, the girls created a confusing cacophony of sound. Waving her arms to quiet them she said, "Okay, okay. What's going on? One at a time!"

Looking over the children, Lenore focused on Darla, figuring the adult would make the most sense. "What is happening?"

"What is happening is that the bride is MIA," Darla said quietly with a great deal of nervousness. "Somewhere in Nashville, there is a beautiful Black woman running the streets in a cream colored Vera Wang."

Lenore was in shock. "What?"

"What's going on?" asked Dexter.

"We can't find Aunt Maggie, sir," said Mary Margaret, pulling on the large man's tux jacket. Suddenly perplexed, she looked at her sister and asked, "Wait. Do we still call her *Aunt Maggie* or *Aunt mom?*"

Gwen rolled her eyes and said, "Shhhh."

"No one has seen her," Dexter asked, directing his question to anyone in the group with an answer.

"No sir," Darla said. "But her dress is gone, and it looks as though she's been getting ready, because all of her make-up and things are kind of strewn about. Oh Lord, I hope nothing's happened to her."

His brow furrowed, Dexter thought for a moment. Locking eyes with his wife, they both knew the one place their only child could be. "Hopefully she has her cell with her," he said as he simultaneously hit the speed dial button for Maggie's number while digging his car keys from his pocket. "How much time do we have," he asked.

"Just over two hours," Lenore said.

"I'm on it," said Dexter. "Say nothing to anyone," he instructed the group. "I will be right back."

"Yes sir," the ladies said in unison.

Chapter 18

The cab driver was only slightly bemused. When he stopped on the corner of Fifth and Broadway, he found the woman in the poofy white dress to be a bit strange, but this was Downtown Nashville; strange was the new black.

As he followed her request and drove her south on Interstate 65, his confusion deepened. She asked him to take her to Franklin. During the ride, she simply stared out the window, a strange, sad smile on her face. Something resembling a blanket was folded neatly on her lap.

Why this woman asked him to take her from Downtown Nashville to Franklin was beyond him, but hey, that dress looked expensive. There might be a really big tip on top of a really big fare.

Suddenly, it dawned on the driver that he'd seen her somewhere before. On television perhaps. Or maybe even in one of those magazines his wife reads. He couldn't quite place it, but he knew her from somewhere. She *had* to be a celebrity of some sort, he reasoned. Only a celebrity would be strange enough to hail a cab in a wedding dress and ask to be taken to a cemetery.

Maggie ignored the call that came from the phone inside her purse. "Turn here please," she said politely.

She knew that people were looking for her. She knew

what she was doing was silly, if not a little unsafe. But through the parties, couples shower, rehearsal, and the things of everyday life in between, there was something burning in Maggie's spirit; a visit she needed to make.

By the time this particular morning dawned, Maggie could ignore that burning no longer. She'd tried to sneak away at sunrise, but got waylaid by her Aunt Sharon and Uncle David, cornering her into coffee and conversation.

She got to the Ryman and proceeded to get dressed. It was during an instant when Tessa had slipped out to take a phone call that she seized her moment. *It's now or never*, she thought. She looked at the clock on the wall. *A couple of hours to spare*. Grabbing her favorite lap blanket, Maggie slipped her cell into her purse, and sneaked out the side door of the building.

"Up here," Maggie said pointing over the front seat. They didn't have to go far. Grace's headstone was under one of the trees near the entrance.

As Maggie got out of the cab, the driver snapped his fingers. "Hey, aren't you…?"

"Nah. But I get that all the time," Maggie playfully fibbed. "Keep things running, if you don't mind? I won't be long."

The driver understood. The edge of his mustache curled slightly upward as he nodded and said kindly, "Sure, lady. No prob."

From the cab to the stone bench, Maggie hiked her dress just enough so that it wouldn't brush the ground. Slowly, she spread the blanket she'd brought with her and sat down.

Inhaling, Maggie simply stared at the photo on the headstone. Time and weather had begun to cause a bit of fading, but the smiles emanating from it were still clearly visible.

"I remember when you took that photo."

Maggie looked up to find the source of the voice.

The cab was gone, and in its place stood a woman in a cobalt blue crepe wool suit. She flipped her sable-brown hair casually over one shoulder in a way Maggie had seen a million times before. "Thanksgiving, right?" Grace asked.

"Yep," Maggie said. "The one that will go down as The Great Turkey Day debacle."

Grace laughed, "Yeah, probably one of the worst food fights in our family's history."

Maggie's eyes narrowed in concern. "Doesn't it seem strange to you that this family has actually had other food fights to compare it to?"

"Seriously?" Grace smirked. "Have we just met?"

"Good point. Well, who started it anyway? I honestly can't remember"

"Can't remember? Matty, of course."

"He starts so many fights, they all just kinda blur together," said Maggie.

"Let me see," Grace said thoughtfully. "If memory serves, M&M tried to tell him what to do. Again."

"Naturally."

"Then he got ticked off and flung a spoonful of mashed potatoes in her hair."

Maggie's eyes widened at the memory. "Oh, that's right, and M&M retaliated, but missed and got it on Joe…"

"Who missed, and somehow got it on Dad and Gwennie at the same time…"

"Then it was total bedlam…"

"Food Fight!" the two women said in unison before laughing aloud.

"If you look closely," Grace said, pointing at the photo

on the headstone, "You can just make out a trace of potato in M&M's hair."

"And I'm pretty sure that's gravy on your sweater," Maggie said on closer inspection.

"You know what? You're right!"

Grace and Maggie stood a few feet apart, silently regarding one another for a few seconds before Grace broke the through the quiet.

"Well, look at you," she said as she walked toward Maggie. "Gettin' married. Anyone I know?" she asked sarcastically.

"Ha ha ha."

The women hugged. Suddenly, Grace pushed back. "Hey. You're stealin' my man. You know, if I weren't dead, I'd totally kill you."

"Do they have you doing stand up in the afterlife?" Maggie asked. "If so, I can't imagine how excruciating that must be for everyone. Your jokes were bad enough down here."

"I try to keep things entertaining. Here, come sit with me."

They returned to the bench as Grace took Maggie's hands in her own. For the briefest of moments, they were 16 again; sharing secrets, talking over problems, cracking more bad jokes. The feeling was wonderfully overwhelming.

"I can't stay long," Maggie said. "I just needed this minute with you. I miss you so much."

"I miss you too. But I'm so proud. So very, very proud of you, Mags."

"None of this seems right without you," Maggie said before remembering the fact that she was dressed to wed her dead friend's husband. "Well, uh...you know what I mean."

Grace laughed. "Yes, I do. But I'm always near. Every time you look into our children's eyes - you'll see me. None of this was accidental. None of it caught God by surprise. Everything you've been through, both good and bad, it was all part of a greater plan. I know that Joe and the rug rats are in safe capable hands - the Lord's...and yours."

Maggie reached up and cupped Grace's cheek in her hand as Grace went on. "Mom and Dad will be fine. Sissy will be more than fine. Even Richard will be okay."

"Not that anyone cares," Maggie said ruefully.

"Aw, you care," Grace said. "That's what makes you wonderful. Regardless of his treatment of you, you still care about him - as a person. Even though he's no longer your responsibility, you do pray for him."

"How do you know I pray for...? Oh, yeah never mind."

"You should know that that kind of stuff does not go unnoticed in my neck of the woods," Grace said. "But you don't need to concern yourself with any of that. Today is about you."

Grace pulled Maggie up off of the bench and, fingers intertwined, they stretched their arms out wide. "Thank you Mags. Thank you for taking care of things. Thank you for being the best friend I've ever had in life, and even in death. Thank you for loving my family the way that you have."

"Oh, I miss you," Maggie cried as the two of them embraced once again.

"You'll see me again. Not any time soon, mind you."

"Thank heavens for that...I mean..."

"I know what you meant, and you're right. You're at

the start of an amazing journey. Relish it. All of it. You're going to be celebrated all over the world. *Finally*! But don't miss the little moments that make life grand. That is where Joe and the kids come in. Love them with everything you have, as you always do. That will be more fulfilling than anything else."

"Family is everything," Maggie said knowingly.

"Family is everything," Grace repeated.

Grace took a long look at the world she'd left behind. "I'm not really supposed to miss anything. This is my Eternal Reward, after all," she said, gesturing with a flourish. "But if there were anything I'd love to experience again, it would be your friendship."

"Just something to which we can both look forward," Maggie said.

"But not any time soon," they said together again as they laughed.

A tear rolled down Maggie's cheek, releasing her from her imagination. She rose from the bench, exhausted and exhilarated from the supernatural conversation. She bent down, pressed her fingers to her lips, and then gently touched Grace's image. "Thank you sweetie," she whispered. "I love you." She then picked up a rock and placed it on top of the stone.

"Why did you leave that rock there?"

Although startled at the sound of her father's voice, Maggie didn't jump. She simply looked to see him standing in the spot where her heart saw Grace just a few moments before.

With the cab driver paid and kindly dismissed, Dexter walked over to Maggie. Looping her arm through his, she began her explanation.

"Our road manager was raised Jewish. He said that his

mother told him, 'flowers die, rocks do not...so it's the most permanent way to let the departed know you were there.'"

"Gotcha," Dexter said.

"Are we late," Maggie asked. "Wait, more important...how did you know I was here?"

"You might not believe this, but I know you better than you think I do."

Maggie blushed. "No, I believe it. I'm sorry I went AWOL. I woke up this morning with this feeling in my gut that if I didn't come here, things wouldn't feel complete. I needed this trip to...I don't know...bring everything full circle, I guess."

"*Everything comes full circle...*" Dexter started to sing. Maggie was astounded that her father knew her song. He continued in a rich baritone as he walked her back to his car.

"It falls together in the end
The unshakable truth that save my life
Is that you are my best friend...

"Daddy..." Maggie said, her shock deepening as he sang.

"You really don't think I know you, do you, child?" he said, helping her in the car. He dusted the grass from the edges of her gown as he piled the yards of satin and tulle around her.

"I guess not," she said, ashamed. "I'm sorry."

"My daughter has a song on the County, Pop and R&B charts for a couple of months, and that song won her a Grammy Award? C'mon! It's something a dad doesn't tend to miss, if he's a good dad."

"You are, Daddy. I'm really sorry."

Dexter rounded the car quickly to respond to his daughter. "No baby. *I'm* sorry," he said as he settled into the driver's seat. "I'm sorry it's taken me this long to realize what Matt and Janice, even your own mother understood. Our children need to be celebrated. When they've chosen their road, it might not jive with what we want, but if it's worthwhile…"

He started the car, but sat thoughtfully before driving away. "One thing I remember about Grace - she was one of the happiest children I'd ever seen. Everyone was drawn to her. And you."

"Moth to flame," Maggie said, smiling. "I know."

"But at the heart of that happiness was the fact that Matt and Janice really let her run free with her art. If she had a dream, they'd watch her pursue it, and she had great success in her life. They never dismissed her, or wrote her off, or…tried to change her. They loved her for who she was…" His voice broke as the revelations continued.

"Dad," Maggie said softly. She took his hand and squeezed. "It's okay. We're here now. And it's okay. Now quit crying or you're gonna make me cry!"

Dexter laughed. "Just let me get this out, okay? I *celebrate* you, Mary Margaret West. I do, my baby. There was never a time that I didn't support you. I just know what kind of world it is. And I didn't want to see that world swallow you up. But in being practical, I guess, well, I lost sight of things. I was trying to protect you, but I ended up making you feel *less than*. And for that, my sweet girl, I am eternally sorry."

Maggie was deeply moved. Beyond words. Pulling the borrowed and blue handkerchief from her purse, she dabbed at her eyes. "Thank you Daddy."

The large black sedan pulled out onto Hillsboro Pike

and headed north to Nashville. His judicial sternness and fatherly concern returned. "Now, call your mother and tell her we're on our way."

"Yes sir," she said.

Chapter 19

Dexter pulled his car into the south alley alongside the Ryman. At the end of the alley was Fourth Street, where a steady stream of invitation-only wedding guests, tourists and the occasional street person could be seen. Downtown Nashville had been brought to a near-standstill to accommodate the limousines depositing stars of every stripe and genre onto the red carpet that Deana insisted lead up to the entrance of the venue. The flurry of activity was sufficient enough distraction for Maggie to slip in under the public radar.

"There you go, honey. Safe and sound," Dexter said.

"Talk about insanity," Maggie said in disbelief. "Now you know, none of this is me, right? Had it been up to me and Joe, we'd be on a beach somewhere with just you guys, the kids, and our pastors."

"Followed by a barbecue and really bad volleyball," added Dexter.

They laughed.

"Amen to that!" she said. "Well, it's a beautiful day, so let's just soldier on through this dog and pony show that my former boss so kindly paid for."

Dexter touched his forehead to Maggie's. "You know, the fact that she's paying is the best part about this whole thing."

As Maggie gave her father a playful shove, her

bridesmaids along with Gwen and Mary Margaret rounded the corner; all equally excited to see that Maggie had returned unharmed. She couldn't help but laugh at the rapid-fire succession of comments and questions from the small mob.

"A-*mazing* how you kept this dress from becoming a total disaster," Tessa said as she gave Maggie a full inspection.

"Tessa, chill," Maggie said calmly. "Everything is going to be fine. I took a little road trip. It was something I needed to do. This wasn't a cold feet thing. Take it down a notch, okay?"

It seemed as though several extra hands immediately sprang from the young woman; with sponges and brushes in hand, Tessa began dabbing and powdering Maggie's makeup. Her movements were fast and furious, yet simultaneously light to the touch. "Thank goodness you're wearing your hair pulled back," she continued, more to herself than to anyone else.

"Whoa, wow, warn me first before you start attacking me with those things," Maggie said, trying to keep the atmosphere humorous and upbeat.

Tessa continued to mumble in her semi-cognizant state. "I don't know what we'd be doing at this late hour..."

"Young lady," Lenore said, gently laying her hand on Tessa's arm. The action seemed to bring the girl back to Earth. "This is my daughter's day, not yours," Lenore said. "If she went down the aisle in her pajamas, she'd be fine. So that will be enough of the fussing. Okay?"

Tessa nodded meekly as Maggie stifled an expression of amusement. "Like you'd ever let me go down the aisle looking anything less than completely hooked up," Maggie said softly to her mother. Lenore touched her cheek to her daughter's as the two giggled.

"Now, we still have a few minutes while the guests are still being seated outside," Maggie said calmly. Holding out her hands, she looked at Joe's daughters. "If you all will excuse me, I'd like to have a word with my girls."

Maggie led Gwen and Mary Margaret back to her dressing room. She sat down in front of the mirror, and began to secure the silk floral headpiece to her chignon. The blusher cascaded down her back like a tulle fountain. As Maggie gazed on them with one of her sweetest smiles, the girls marveled.

"Wow," Gwen said. "You look like a total princess, Aunt…" She stopped short. "We can't call you Aunt Maggie now, can we?"

Maggie turned to face them. "You can't?"

This time, it was Mary Margaret's turn to speak. "I wanted to call you Aunt Mom, but Gwennie thought that was stupid."

"It *is* stupid, M&M," Gwen said, giving her customary roll of the eyes.

The exchange was the same as it had ever been, but there was something to the girl's mini-spat that felt like a new and open door to Maggie. Somehow, she couldn't wait for the rest of her life to unfold. She wasn't living solely for herself any longer; these young women, as well as Matty, were now her charges. She wasn't just the baby sitter, the friend of their mother. She *was* the mother now.

Yet another bittersweet revelation that caused Maggie's eyes to well up.

"You know what?" she said as she dabbed at her eyes again. "If Aunt Maggie is the most comfortable way to address me for now, that's okay…because as far as I am concerned, you have a mom. Her name is Grace. And she will always be with us. And if you do decide to start calling me Mom, trust me, I am fairly confident that she'll be okay with that. She knows you won't ever forget her."

Carefully, the girls encircled their arms around Maggie and lightly embraced her.

"We can call you anything we want," Mary Margaret asked.

"Yep," said Maggie. "Well, 'stepmonster' is out of the question, but pretty much everything else is okay."

"A red carpet, Dee?"

As their limo pulled into its designated spot, Charles was quick to voice his disgust. "This ain't the dad-gum CMA's, woman," he said as he reached for the door handle. "I knew I shouldn't have let you plan this thing. It's enough we're payin' for the Ryman. You've gone too far this time!"

"Charles," Deana said as she placed her hand over his to stop him. "You have steered the course of my career beautifully. I owe you so much. But the one thing I'll never be able to stomach is the thought of you bullying Maggie into thinking she couldn't make it on her own. It wasn't just a slap in her face; it was a slap in mine."

"Can we talk about this later? We've gotta go, we're holdin' up the line. Now screw on your smile, and let's hit it."

"See, this is what I'm talking about," Deana said. "You need to shut up and let me have my say, for once in your life!"

In shock at her telling him to 'shut up,' Charles sat back in his seat and said nothing.

"We will hold up the line, because I am payin' for this

line," she said. "Me. My name, and my reputation...*and* my talent. You seem to forget that little truth most of the time. That yes, it is your business savvy that keeps us rolling, but it's *my* voice the people wanna hear. And when you decided that I was little to nothing without Maggie, well that's when I had just about enough of your mess. This shindig ain't just for her, although Heaven knows we owe her at least that. This day is for me too."

The two of them sat quietly as the crowd continued its frenzy in anticipation of who just might be inside.

"This was my way of saying, well, that I'm more than just the face of this team we've manufactured for the world. It was my way of takin' some sort of control back," she said quietly.

Charles wished that they'd found another time to get to the heart of their matters, but he did understand.

"I get that," he replied. "And I promise you we'll talk about it later. For real. But for now, let's get goin' okay?"

He took her hand and kissed it with a sincerity she'd not seen from him in some time.

"Okay," she said.

Flashbulbs were cracking at lightning speed at the sight of Deana and Charles as they exited their limousine. The switch flipped, and Dee instantaneously became Deana Timmons.

"Deana, is there any truth to the rumor that Maggie's bringing her band to co-headline your next tour," asked one reporter.

"How do you feel about her beating you out at the Grammys and the American Music Awards?" chimed another.

"Do you think she'll become an Opry member this year?"

"People, people," Charles cut in. "Just because the

wedding is being held at the Mother Church of Country Music doesn't mean this is an industry thing."

"Absolutely," Deana said with her megawatt smile. "As you all know, we here in TimmonsLand are all about *Family First*, right? Well, the future Mrs. Maggie Buchanan has always been, and always will be, family. We couldn't be happier for all her success!"

"So as her family, we wanted to make sure she had the best place possible to start this new chapter of her life," Charles continued. "Deana is still the Queen. But Maggie, well, Maggie's our princess. And she and her Jim deserve a royal setting for their big day. We wish 'em both nothin' but the best."

"Joe," Deana said out of the side of her mouth.

Charles gave her a look of confusion. "What?"

"The man's name is *Joe*," said Deana, her smile still affixed for the cameras. "At least learn the man's name."

Charles gave a hearty laugh. "Oh Dee, I keep forgettin' that joke's only funny 'mongst the four of us," he lied. Looking at the bank of cameras, microphones and reporters, he winked and said, "I just wanted to make sure ya'll were payin' attention."

Maggie could hear the music begin Pachabel's *Canon in D*. She had created a special arrangement of the song, and combined it with a song she'd known since childhood, "Seek Ye First," to create a beautiful counter melody. As the choruses combined, Maggie knew that the mothers were being seated.

In her mind's eye, she could see Joe standing at the base of the stage steps with Declan and the other groomsmen. She could see him nervous and excited. She chuckled at the thought of Matty squirming in discomfort at having to wear his little tuxedo.

She stood and finally looked at herself in full. Chantilly lace with a sweetheart neckline covered the bodice, with intricate beadwork. The skirt was cream colored silk with matching lace and beadwork at the bottom. Her train attached, she raised her chin to accentuate the pearls that rested beautifully around her neck.

"Eat your heart out, Kate Middleton," she said to herself, smiling.

"Alright honey, it's time to..." Dexter paused, overcome with delight. The sight of his daughter in her full regalia stopped him mid-sentence. He cleared his throat. "You look absolutely stunning," he said.

"Thanks, Daddy."

"You ready?"

"Yep," she said. "Let's go."

The occasion called for a grand entrance. One that could only be made from the rarely opened doors that led to Fourth Street. As Dexter and Maggie waited for the musical cue, the gathered crowd outside began to cheer for their new hometown heroine.

Feeling regal, Maggie turned and waved to the multitude, whose adoration now reached near fever pitch.

"Okay," Dexter said. "Here we go."

As the doors opened slowly, the entire auditorium stood upon seeing Maggie and her father make their way down the aisle. Joe adjusted his tie just as he caught sight of his bride. The joy and wonder in his face were undeniable. Even before Maggie and Dexter found their way to the bottom of the platform stairs, there was hardly a dry eye in the house.

There would be many things about that day of which
Maggie would need to be reminded: for a bride to
remember every detail of her special day was a rare thing.
But this moment she would hold in her heart forever. Joe's
adoration. Matty remaining miraculously well-behaved.
The glow that came from the faces of Gwen and Mary
Margaret. The pride of her parents. And the chill that rose
from her fingertips to her soul the moment Joe took her
hand.

But the deepest thrill she would know was her final,
precious moment with Grace, a moment that only she and
her parents would ever know or discuss in life. The
blessing and approval she received from that time at
Grace's grave might have, in reality, only been in her
imagination; but it reminded Maggie of the unconditional
love that was born between the two women. A love that
Maggie would carry throughout her marriage to Joe. A love
that she would share with her new family as a mother. A
love that she would infuse into her music for the rest of her
days.

It was a love that truly brought everything in her life
full circle.

Also available from:

WordCrafts Press

Maggie's Song - Full Circle, Volume 1
by Marcia Ware

www.wordcrafts.net